I0712683

By the Way

The Tales Fairies Tell About Us

Holly Walters

with Contributions and art by: Adam Wassil

TLS

Table of Contents

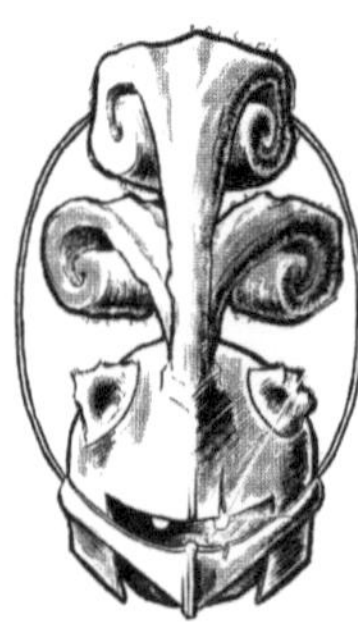

Dedication

OPPOSITE TEA

I've invited my shadow to tea,
He sits opposite me, and as I am
Pulling skin from chapped lips to drop in for sugar
He laments that I am second-born,
Awake, alive, this Tenth Plague morn.

Through porcelain-riddled cracks,
He usually lacks the capacity to see
The words etched in rose leaves and fissure
Saying I was spared both thorn and crown,
By meager clothes lying 'round.

My shadow comes to tea,
Though he and I do not agree, that when
Trees no longer age enough to root the moor
We cannot rely upon their faith,
As we burn their souls to the wraith.

So, he beckons me back to books,
The very trees he mistook for Philo's prose
As Rome cuts stones to entomb the world.
I eat my cakes, toast to my utter nonsense friend,
And drink together to our end.

In German, Eigengrau means 'intrinsic grey': The name for the broadly uniform darkness people see in the absence of light. Or, it is a kind of dark-light hallucination from behind closed eyes because the mind is simply incapable of seeing nothing. For some, it is merely a place of solitude and quiet before sleep. For others, an expanse of the terrifyingly infinite with possibilities for all manner of dreams, nightmares, and imagination.

It was also the name of a pond.

And for three years, Emily Pendleton's father had taken her down to the Eigengrau to 'bury' her goldfish. She'd loved them desperately — despite not a one lasting longer than a few months — but consignment to a cardboard shoe box in the back garden was simply not good enough. They needed to go home, she insisted, and that was surely not into the dirt.

Now, wrapped in sticky paper towels, Comet, the formerly bi-colored fantail, was set to join the others in the memorial waters of a backwoods marsh whose name was just as much of a statement on her current mood as it was the embodiment of a child's thoughts on a goldfish's life after death.

Emily was grateful that she wasn't alone this time though, because her father had opted not to come along.

He hadn't since just after she'd turned nine, giving his regrets and excuses in the form of a blanket dismissal. It was just another fish, he'd said. Ordinary and generally useless.

Even so, Emily didn't see why that should mean she should treat them as any less. A person, after all, is a tyrant over the life of a goldfish. Carving out the smallest spaces. Dropping them into the bowl of a glass vase to feed on dry crumbs, and to die just as quickly as the cut blossoms that would likely follow them.

They remain still and serene only because they cannot breathe, so they simply float by on flimsy wings and wait for nothing. The life he could have offered them was vast and unfathomable, but he didn't. Because they were common.

But Hannalore understood her sorrow. Hannalore was always there to comfort her.

Near the shore, a few cracked stalks rattled in the breeze. It could have been reeds, or it could have been bones, but the tangled strands of black hair that pulled through the weave of the thatched swamp were readily recognizable.

The face that lifted from the muck to peer up at her with papery skin and a white cicada's eyes was almost human, if not for the roots that grew throughout its mummified features. And then there were the raven's claw arms that steadied its rise. Today, Hannalore wore a tattered sort of dress that Emily had seen a few times before.

It was yellowed and badly stained, with a knit so wide it caught the falling grass seeds wherever the spindly figure passed through the tussocks. Pieces of an old limestone grave marker, complete with carved cherubic faces, sat upon an angular wreath made of woven flower-vines which was tied precariously on the creature's head like a macabre crown. But Emily was happy to see her friend all the same, even when dressed for a funeral.

She carefully unwrapped the lifeless goldfish and held it up to Hannalore's approach.

"I don't know what I did wrong." She said, stifling a sob. "Why do they always die no matter what I do?"

Gently folding slender limbs into a crouched and vaguely sitting position, her friend turned to contemplate the fading orange scales and motionless, heavily-lipped, mouth.

"Sometimes, it is the things we cannot do that are the most painful for us to endure, Emily. We cannot give what we do not have."

The voice was an odd combination of soothing and sinister, blending the low timbre of croaking frogs with the hush of swaying trees and water lapping on sand. It wasn't a sound that Emily truly associated with any person she'd ever known but in the preceding months she had come to think of Hannalore as a kind older woman, even as a grandmother of sorts, and always referred to her as such whenever she told her parents about their adventures in the marsh. Stories that were, of course, met with her father's growing concern.

"He won't come here anymore either."

"I know."

The little girl sighed and held out the remains. "Will you keep him with the others? So he won't be alone?"

"Of course. There is a place for everyone."

She laid the bundle into a single offered hand, which curled away and vanished into muddy flesh and gloom.

"Are they OK?"
"They are fine."
"Do they get to swim around and be free?"
"The pond is safe, Emily. They stay in the pond."
"Can I see them?"
"No. They are very far down, and the colors have all gone away now."

Hannalore never left her alone at the side of the pond, so Emily took what comfort she could in a few minutes of silence, but when the mosquitos finally became too much, she stood up.

"Let's go home." She spoke sadly. "I don't want to be here anymore."

Hannalore nodded. "Yes. We will go."

The walk home wasn't long, but the girl dreaded it all the same. Small rural towns were horrific places, not because of what they were but because of what they pretended to be. A nicely mowed lawn and new coats of paint were all it took to hide garish bruises beneath the veneer of a wooden house. But like lipstick on a cut, broken skin was always a little uneven.

Welcoming storefronts implied a ready community, but not the eyes that glared suspiciously from behind the register until a recognized name was offered up in exchange for hospitality. A new sign and a service smile were also sometimes so bright that any diner patron buzzing in at night could easily forget the unsubtle suggestions and threatening stares received from a town where a few modern conveniences or a new truck were the lowest advertised price for the label of a 'good family.'

Emily glanced at the houses that lined her street. They were all old, probably built in the late mid-century for the most part, but reasonably well-kept. They also all had roughly the same shape and design, with what were clearly scattered farmhouses here and there that had been overtaken by the edge of town as it had grown out into the fields.

She saw them as wildflowers to the tract-house weeds; turning their faces into the sun as they faded away beneath benign neglect. Despite the clear summer weather though, Emily only ever saw all of the windows as dark; as hollowed-out voids in the meticulous façade of a lovely neighborhood.

With monstrous shadows quietly holding court within. As if each house had been offered up to imprison its inhabitants within their own personal Hell. But then they had all painted Purgatory white and happily filled it with new souls.

Hannalore bobbed along next to her, her stride the gentle sway of too-tall grass even though she wasn't much over five and a half feet. She also seemed to be now adorned in a simple loose shift and soaked shoes. As she had begun to dry on their walk, her dark hair fell soft and loose to her waist, and her face appeared more dirty than deathless, with a mask of moss and clay. Her eyes though, were never quite right no matter which angle she was seen from.

"I have to go to the doctor tomorrow." Emily said, rather amiably.

"Yes." Was the calm response.

"Will you come with me?"

Hannalore nodded. "Yes, Emily. I said I would."

"Ok. Thank you, Hannalore."
"You're welcome, Button."

TWO

"It's this imaginary friend thing she's got going on, Lana."

Her mother was on the phone again, in the living room, when Emily came in through the back door.

"I mean, when she was five it wasn't a big deal, you know? I had my fair share of imaginary friends at that age. But she's nine. She'll be ten in August, and she's never given up on it. I thought for sure she'd outgrow it by now."

Murmuring on the other side of the line only made her mother sigh deeper. "Ha, ha, but no, she's not possessed. Yes, I know Dale thinks it's funny. I'm taking her to this doctor tomorrow though so, maybe he can figure it out. Feels like more than just a phase, right? I mean, Jenna never had imaginary friends this long. Or, you know, this...detailed."

Emily lingered in the hallway, slowly scuffing her foot against the rug near the stairs.

"You already know what her father thinks." Her mother's strained voice continued. "Yesterday he said it was probably my fault for letting her get away with everything. But I don't! Sure, she spends most of her time wandering around by the lake but there really isn't much for a kid her age to do around here and God knows she never makes any friends."

Hannalore turned and smiled from the dining room archway, playfully tapping a finger against her chin as if to suggest she were contemplating a response to that claim. Emily giggled.

"Emmy? Is that you?"

"Hi Mama. I'm back!"

"Go get washed up before you do anything else, ok? I don't want mud all over the house."

"Ok."

The conversation continued on a minute later in a hurried, hushed tone. "Her goldfish died again yesterday. I really don't get why Neil keeps getting them for her. They just go belly up within the week. And then, of course, she has to march down to the pond every time for a 'funeral.' After that it's nothing but 'Hannalore said this' or 'Hannalore did that.' Unfortunately, humoring her just isn't working.

Maybe Neil's right and it's time to put our foot down about this."

A pause.

"Well, we'll see what the psychologist says. Maybe there's a pill or something."

Standing half-way up the stairs in the no man's land between the overhead banister and an eight-foot drop, Emily made her second determination of the day. Families were horrific. Not because of what they were but because of what they pretended to be.

Her reverie was interrupted when Jenna, her aforementioned older sister, poked her head out from her room. "Hey, Em. What's going on?"

"Nothing. I was just down at the pond."

"Yeah, you really shouldn't do that, you know? I think mom's worried you'll fall in and drown one of these days."

Emily pinched her face in an exaggerated expression of mock annoyance. At sixteen, Jenna had taken on a habit of motherly worrying but lately her method of attributing her concerns to their actual mother, who had never expressed anything of the sort, felt more aggravating than it should.

She was constantly scolding the younger girl not to hang around the pond, not to be out too late, and to be more mannerly; all citing a mother who had rarely even asked either of them how a single school day had been. But on the other hand, Jenna never complained about nor reprimanded her for Hannalore.

"I'm not going to fall in."

"Let me guess. Because Hannalore would catch you?"

Emily scowled. "Because I'm nine and I know how to not fall in the water. It's not even deep."

"Yeah, well, be careful, ok?"

Jenna didn't so much as flinch then when Hannalore herself, her tangled hair catching on her sister's pensive face, slid between them to meander down the hall towards Emily's room. Not that she would have reacted regardless, even though the smaller girl was always somewhat surprised by it. No one else had ever seen Hannalore, or they pretended not to if they did.

Years ago, Emily had once attempted to point her out to everyone who would listen; trying to make them see the watery footprints in the mud or hear the words whispered between her own at the dinner table. But they couldn't and she'd stopped trying. It was still strange to her though, when they didn't even seem to feel what touched them.

Emily turned and trundled down the hall, wiping her hands on her jeans and following Hannalore to the doorway of her room. As was their custom, her friend had already begun the process of fettering out any hidden dangers that might be lurking there, peering under the bed and opening the closet to chase out the monsters. Her long fingers raked at the hanging clothes and battered a few toys away from the wall.

She then lifted the empty fish bowl from the nightstand and returned it to the girl's desk before turning and pronouncing the room safe. Only then would Emily cross the threshold.

She sat down on the bed next to her friend. "If the doctor asks about you tomorrow, what should I say?"

"What do you want to say?"

"They'll think I'm crazy if I tell the truth."

"Yes, that happens to a lot of people, mostly because the truth is usually hard to hear. But they do it anyway."

"Why?"

"Because the truth isn't always for other people. Sometimes it is for you. They do not have to accept it. The gift was not for them anyway."

"I don't know. Seems like I'm the one who gets punished for it."

"We suffer the harms inflicted upon us, not because we deserve it, Button. But because they are inescapable. We are not what is done to us."

Emily actually smiled at that. "So, you're saying I should tell them about you."

"You should tell them about you. If I am a part of that, what objection could I have?"

"Hey! Em!" Jenna padded to a stop outside her sister's door and peeked in. "Food. Let's go."

"Is dad home?"

"Not yet. Why?"

"No reason."

Emily looked up to Hannalore, who still sat partially leaning to one side and teetering unsteadily on a spine that wasn't bound up quite tightly enough. "Are you coming down?"

"I'm afraid not, Button. I have work to do now."

Jenna, quite used to precisely this exchange from the past several months, only impatiently tapped her socked feet on the hardwood to remind everyone that she was there and waiting.

Emily nodded. "What are you doing tonight?"

"Fetching your new goldfish."

THREE

Neil Pendleton was a handsome man, though it had ultimately done very little for him. A fine face might be small-town currency at the height of adolescence, but as soon as he had begun approaching forty it was more of a conversational after-thought over beers in the back yard. Now, it was just better that he usually came home late at night so that no one, least of all himself, could see what he was doing to the refined features and strong jawline in his yearbook photos.

The house was quiet save for the hum of the bedroom air conditioner somewhere far overhead. But he stood motionless in the hallway, staring solemnly up the stairs and listening to the sound of blood rushing in his ears as the world struggled not to tilt.

Beer hadn't been enough to drown him this time, so he'd switched to the harder shelf. He'd still managed to make it through the front door though, and was contemplating the next challenge that would get him as close as possible to his pillow.

It was better than sleepwalking, if not appreciably different and as Neil finally focused long enough to be able to see the ascending staircase, he balked at the moving shadows. The faces in the family photos turned away from him as a beam of reflected light from a passing car raced through the house. Just behind it, in the spaces where there was no light and no contrast, he swore something else turned back to look at him.

Some composite creature with arms made of cracked balusters that dangled from underneath a pile of discarded clothes had appeared to celebrate his return, as usual. And then he laughed. The third stair creaked on his way up. On the eighth, he kicked a forgotten tube of glitter lip balm off the edge. By the landing, he had managed to steady himself just enough not to crash into the wall and risk waking everyone up, even though his steps were becoming heavier, more like the pulse throbbing in his head.

But blessedly, the bed was in sight only a few feet ahead. With a relieved sigh, Neil flipped off his shoes, stumbled, pulled at his belt and pants, and then simply gave up and shoved his way under the duvet. His wife stirred but said nothing aside from a resigned noise.

Honestly, he didn't care. The ceiling was already slowly blurring into a wash of calm surface ripples. His mind was descending into the depths of unconsciousness, and the dizzying roll of intoxication made him still. On a whim, he reached one hand up to play at the floating spots wafting through his vision. They were probably just pressure flashes, but the dancing lights reminded him of a childhood spent at the carnival.

He could see all the little cups of fish lined up to be won as prizes on the midway. Just toss a ball in the bowl and get a sad golden minnow for your dollar. But then he'd find them abandoned in the field behind the Tilt-a-Whirl and on the curb of the street as he walked home. Most of them dead already and forgotten, floating limply in less than a handful of water. For a moment, he thought of it all rather fondly. So much so, that he smiled...

...when another hand broke through the shallows and entwined into his.

It was an uncanny sort of dream that followed but what made it all the worse was that he had been having this same dream for years. No matter how much he tried to avoid it, no matter how much he steeped his brain in drink, it always came back. Always. And it did so now with a brutal vengeance.

He was fighting, though the terror he felt was thick with exhaustion. A crushing weight settled over his chest; the sleep, the drink, and a black-mouthed shape, joined the unmovable stones he had only piled upon himself. He tasted rust and felt the sharp nails that picked at the skin of his chapped lips, grinding grass and mud between his teeth until he was forced to gape for air. Which he did since he could do nothing else. Neil thrashed and struggled, unsure if his own body was even real anymore or if it was just an idea that he had of one.

But it was the face in the water that froze his heart, shivering behind his ribs as he watched it swim down to him from somewhere far, far, above. He choked but the hands at his lips were insistent; ever prying, and scratching, and scraping until the lump in his throat rose so high, he thought he would vomit. Something squirmed in his mouth and the fingers pulled again. His body heaved. He wanted to scream and would have if not for the tumbling in his gullet that swallowed it up.

Though, almost as soon as he thought he would suffocate for certain, the writhing agony finally ended. The flopping horror was snatched free from his tongue. He coughed and thought he might have moaned as the spare silhouette carefully cupped a flash of golden-bright glimmer in its meager hands. Afterwards, it bowed with mock reverence and little sense of dignity, barely acknowledging his instinctual reach to retrieve whatever it was.

It left him there, floundering, until the stupor was finally enough to overcome him. Until he passed out into a fitful, dreamless nothingness that was already enough of a reason for him to never want to sleep again. And he stayed there for all the time it took the sun to start threatening the integrity of the thin blinds and his closed eyelids at the same time.

Still, in that in-between state, in the greyness of waking that isn't precisely awareness and isn't completely numb, he wandered back out into the hallway again. It was as if he had only now arrived home, and the night had neither passed nor had ever come. Heat prickled his arms, and the artificial cold of the window units annoyed him.

There was an unpleasant taste of bitterness, and perhaps acid, caught in his head that burnt his breath. Just before dawn, Neil Pendleton stopped by his youngest daughter's room to look in on her. And to wonder about the goldfish swimming in slow circles in the bowl on her desk.

FOUR

"Hi, Emily, I'm Dr. Kyteler."
"Hi."
"Is it OK if we talk for a little while?"
"Sure."

Emily appraised the seated figure across from her. Somewhat less interesting than the rich chocolate tones of the room surrounding them, Dr. Kyteler was illuminated beneath a floor lamp in the shape of a ship's beacon, holding a pen in the yielding manner of a white flag.

Everything about him made the girl think of a very inquisitive squirrel, from the tufts of hair that stuck out above his ears to the peculiar angle of his reading glasses that made his eyes look too far apart. He also sat with a posture that elongated his neck and arched his shoulders, leaving plenty of room for her to imagine a big, bushy tail twitching in place of the widely curved chair back. Her friend chuckled lightly next to her.

"How are you doing today, Emily?"

"Fine, I guess."
"Yeah? Anything in particular on your mind?"
She glanced at Hannalore, seated demurely on her right with hands folded in her lap, and wondered just how forthright she should be.

"Not really."

"Can you tell me about yourself? Do you have any pets?"

"Umm. I have a goldfish."

Emily did not register the gentle purse of Dr. Kyteler's eyebrows at this. "Does he or she have a name?"

"Not yet. I just got it."

"Just now?"
"This morning." She replied brightly.

"And who got you your goldfish?"
She paused, but only momentarily, having already made her decision a day earlier. "Hannalore."

He seemed slightly surprised at this, as if hopeful but unexpectant. "Oh? Who's Hannalore, Emily?"

"I…" But Emily was unsure. "She's…my friend."

"Can you tell me about her?"

"Well, I guess. I mean, she's not like a regular friend and…most people don't like it when I talk about her."
"Why is that?"
"They say she's not real. And I shouldn't make stuff up like that."

"Do they sometimes tell you that Hannalore is in your imagination?"
"Yeah."
"Is she real to you, Emily?"

In that question mark lay the riddle of her life. Hannalore sat not more than two feet away from her, as solid and as present as the beacon lamp, the couch, and the doctor.

But nothing in the room, other than her, acted as if any other entity existed but the obvious two. The cushion did not dip or wrinkle, the light did not refract into an extra shadow, and the eager psychologist did not glance elsewhere or flinch reflexively. What Emily saw was a world that no one else did, and she knew it.

Taking the brief silence in stride, Kyteler continued. "Does Hannalore talk?"
"Yes, of course she does."

"Is she talking right now?"
"No."
"Is she here?"
"Yes."
"Where is she?"
"Sitting right there." She waved her hand vaguely over the empty space next to her.

"Is she just here to watch us? Keeping an eye on things? Is that what's going on?"
"Hannalore doesn't talk to other people. She only talks to me."

"Why is that?"
"Because no one else can hear her. Or see her." This caused Emily a moment of sadness and frustration.

The doctor gentled. "Emily, do people get mad at you because of what you see? Do mom and dad get mad at you?"

"Mom says I'm too old for imaginary friends. Dad just thinks…" Hannalore rose from her place on the couch and immediately drifted over to where the psychologist sat, leaning over his shoulder at an impossibly painful slant to peer down at the pen and paper in his lap. This much caused Emily to pause as her gaze tracked the sudden movement.

"Dad thinks?" Dr. Kyeteler prompted.

"That, um, I'm just being difficult, he said. That I just want attention. And it makes things harder for everyone with my nonsense."

A pointed nail stretched out to peel back the first page. The strange, gangly apparition continued to observe whatever was taking place on the notepad with a marked interest. Emily was finding it nearly torture to tear her eyes away from her friend and focus back to the conversation at hand.

"Are you OK, Emily? Something wrong?"

"I'm OK. Hannalore is just...walking around right now and I wanted to see where she was going." It was a little bit of a lie and a little bit of the obscured truth.

"Oh? Where is she now?"

"Um. Looking at your notepad."

Kyeteler actually smiled. "Ah, I see. Worried I'm writing something bad about you?"

When Hannalore spoke. "Not at all. Rather, I find your feigned objectivity banal and tedious. You have ignored all that is truly interesting here."

"I think she just called you boring."

The psychologist chuckled. "You know, that's not the first time I've heard that. But it's definitely the first time I've been called boring by an imaginary friend."

"She's.... She's not imaginary, Dr. Kyeteler. Hannalore is real. She lives in the pond near my house. Everything that dies goes there. Like my goldfish. All my goldfish go there. My dad goes there. No one understands why I have to go there, too."

For the first time in many years, Armin Kyeteler was surprised but equally dismayed. The little girl with the dusty blonde hair and unicorns on her shoes was in crisis but she stared it down as if it were merely the case that Christmas had come late, and she had already stopped believing in Santa Claus. He could feel the pain in her voice, the palpable misery that once again caused her to look away from him and at the wall beyond.

Hannalore nodded in unseen agreement and whispered into his ear from her vantage point leaning on the arm of the chair. "It's because my words aren't big enough to not fall through the cracks. But down there, they find others that people have dropped and forgotten. They mix with mud.

They grow but get stepped on. They can't stand up. So, they come back the next year. And again, the year after that. Until there is no one left to trample them. Then, they cannot be ignored any longer."

FIVE

The worst thing about listening to her parents argue at night was that Emily could only hear bits and pieces of the shouted exchange; the rest had to be interpreted through several layers of walls and flooring until it became a frightful mishmash of vague accusations and misunderstood threats. This time, however, she could distinctly make out the central question that had prompted this round of screaming.

"Why did you get her another goldfish?!"

"I didn't!" Neil countered. "She must have gotten it from somewhere else!"

"Oh no. You came stumbling home last night. Again. And there it is. I wouldn't be surprised if you just forgot about it like the last one. You can't just get her a fish every time the one before it dies. It doesn't fix anything!"

"Oh? And your little trip to the shrink did?"

An exasperated sigh followed. "It was just an evaluation, Neil. We haven't even talked about treatment yet. And you're changing the subject."

"Look, I don't know what your problem is, Kelly. There's nothing wrong with Em. You're probably just making her anxious with all this crap about imaginary friends. She's a kid and kids talk about stupid stuff all the time."

"That's not what's going on here and you know it."

Emily turned over under the blankets and pressed the pillow to her head. It was at times like this that she often took to scraping words into her skin to distract herself from the noise. Using her fingernail, she would dig red questions into her arms. Sometimes, Hannalore would even answer, more words appearing in raised welts across her body, but it was always temporary.

She hated how the real and concrete responses she could finally read there would heal and fade, and then be out of reach again. Briefly, she thought about scratching 'make them stop' onto the back of her hand but she had an uncomfortable sense that her friend wasn't currently with her near enough to read it.

The goldfish flicked its tail and gasped at the surface of the bowl.

"This is about you and your whole 'following in your father's footsteps' bullshit. Or whatever family legacy crap that you've been hung up on since you were a kid. You have two wonderful, beautiful daughters, Neil! Why can't you see that?!"

"There are just some things you don't understand. You'll never understand. There are some things a man can only give to his son. It just means something..."

"I can't believe you sometimes. Considering that your father was just as much of a..."

"Don't start, Kelly. Don't even go there right now."

"Go there? We're way past there. Let's talk about what you're giving Jenna and Emily, why don't we?"

"She has everything she wants. Food, a good house, toys, whatever. Better than I ever had."

"Oh? And maybe if she had some real love and stability in her life, maybe she wouldn't have to invent people to care about her!"

A glass shattered against a wall and the sounds only grew louder, though now much less coherent. Minutes later, a door slammed in response and for a time, the house grew quiet. But then the footsteps followed, a peculiar beat that Emily knew by heart and could predict with unerring accuracy.

The soft, muted creaks of her father pretending that he wasn't skipping the weakest stairs or the broken boards on the landing was almost like a guessing game. A series of rounds she always won. Because he came the same way he always did, up the steps, around the balustrade, past the crumbling plaster on the corner and down the hall in the pattern nearest to silence.

She pulled the blankets over her head and squeezed her eyes shut, hoping that she'd appear asleep. She was so consumed with that hope however, that she didn't notice the faint tap of dripping water onto her rug.

Neil Pendleton stole quietly into his daughter's room. He was angry, his mind in an uncontrolled retch of chaos. Vomiting all the trash it had consumed over the years back up into his soul. He told himself he didn't know what he was doing, while the voice of his own father booming in his head repeated the same thing.

It also told him that what he saw wasn't real; not a girl bundled-up, frightened, beneath her covers but a scene from his own childhood memories after the marks from the belt strap had turned to scars. He was too soon convinced it was all a dream anyway. He wasn't standing in her room, in the middle of the night, contemplating all the things that came to him at times like these.

The girl was just a persistent reminder of his failures, after all, and the goldfish a tailor-made figment mocking his lack of resolve. So, what then, he thought, might the tall figure in the threadbare clothes be? Was it odd that it moved like erratic droplets on a window and drank from an empty fishbowl?

In a singular moment, everything stopped. He had only known fear like this rarely in his life and Neil took a step backwards towards the door again in an involuntary gesture of self-defense. Cold terror gripped him, but he still couldn't make sense of the nightmare. Or, at least, what simply had to be a nightmare.

He needed to wake up but soon found, as before, he could no longer move. Rather, it felt as though he were swimming through weeds that wrapped around his arms and ankles, pulling him down further into darkness. Flashes of gold and red raced through his vision and he thought for certain he was about to be sick.

It was holding him again, plucking at his mouth with dry, insistent fingers. He thought it wanted his screams, but he had long sworn to himself that he would not give them. So, he clenched his teeth and prepared to fight his way out.

"Let go of me." He hissed. "Get your...get your hand...out...of...my..."

He spat and thrashed, cutting his lip on a sharp nail at the end of a finger hooked around his tongue. He lashed out but found nothing to fill his hands but wet, heavy muck until it was as if his entire body was seized beneath a deluge and then went numb. The voices and memories wandered away and Neil shivered as he stumbled out of Emily's room and back into the hall.

When he squinted back towards the pile of bedclothes and his daughter, his attention was momentarily arrested. Nothing in the room had moved, nothing breathed, not even the creature that hung, lifeless, at the surface of the glass on her desk.

Another dead goldfish for Emily to take to the pond.

SIX

Dragging the blue crayon across the paper, Emily completed the second square shape that made up the body of her rather curious rendition of the concept of hope. As Dr. Kyeteler looked on in genial silence, she then picked up a nearby brown pencil to finish the two loops that formed its ears. In all, hope, in this case, looked very much like a rabbit-eared, rainbow-colored, pony being ridden by a garden gnome but, as Emily then went on to explain, the small figure astride the beast was actually her sister.

"Not you?" Kyteler asked.

"No," Emily replied, curling her arm to better color in the sharp angle of the grass beneath hope's three-toed feet. "It's Jenna. She needs it more than me."

"Why is that?"

"Well," she started, before her eyes momentarily flicked to a low, flat chest of toys and back again to her drawing. "She's mostly alone all the time and I wish she could have friends."

"You mean, like Hannalore?"

Emily was uncomfortable. "I guess." She replied and glanced back over to the chest; her line of sight then following a trail of miscellaneous objects to where a small pile of them had formed into a tableau of stuffed frogs and teddy bears at war with a battlement of dolls. A subtle rearrangement by a figure that her psychologist had not seemed to notice.

When she did not resume her coloring, however, he turned in the direction of her gaze. "What's wrong, Emily? Do you see something over there?"

"No. It's nothing."

"Doesn't seem like nothing. You can tell me, you know. It's OK."

"I can't this time. You wouldn't understand. But don't feel bad. No one ever really understands."

The problem wasn't people generally, she wanted to tell him, only in what they pretended to be. That the veneer of the person they offered up to you was just as quickly donned for the present moment as their clothing, their manner, or their smiles.

Or that the reality of her conversations with the weeds and water was just as solid as the exchange she was having now, in the playroom adjacent to his office. Or with her parents at the dining room table. Or Hannalore. And more so, that the consequences of those conversations were what was actually true.

Ultimately, in Emily's thinking, where the other voice was coming from was immaterial in comparison to what the words could do to you, and the words she was keeping now were better left at the bottom of a pond and not with a doctor, where they could do so much more harm than before.

"I'm pretty smart." Dr. Kyeteler smiled. "I might understand better than you know."

"You shouldn't, though." She stated abruptly, looking up from her drawing and staring at him with a wide, worried expression as she nearly crushed the crayon in her palm. "Otherwise, you might see what Hannalore is doing."

Armin Kyeteler was rarely at a loss for words. So, the ones that followed came out almost automatically.

"What is Hannalore doing?"

Emily turned and looked through the open door and back out into the room with the chairs and the desk and the beacon-like lamp layering too many shadows onto the brown décor.

There, she saw her friend, kneeling in the center of the therapy couch, slowly peeling strands of hair and lint from the depths of the cushioned back and placing them into her mouth to chew and swallow with notable relish.

She ate each piece carefully, one by one, with a mouth stretched too wide to be human and teeth that had taken on the look of hooks and needles. The girl shivered but couldn't look away.

"Sitting on your couch."

"Waiting for her session?"
It was a joke, but Emily's response was anything but amused. "No. Cleaning up after the last one, I think."

"What do you mean?"
"Hannalore says that our thoughts leak out of us all the time. We're dropping them all over the place wherever we go. That they get into things. Like water soaking into the carpet when you spill it. That's why places are so important, and where we put our stuff, and what we keep and what we don't.

She said that's why you can feel it when something bad has happened in somewhere when you walk in. Because of all the words that have got in to it and then stayed there."

"Have bad words gotten into your house, Emily?"

"My dad." She said, frowning down at the drawing beginning to wrinkle in her hand. "Sometimes. I think he has bad thoughts that are getting out.

They're sad and then sometimes they're angry but even when he doesn't talk about them, I don't like that it gets into everything. When I was little, I used to get really scared. Not anymore, though...I don't know. Hannalore takes them away when they get too close."

"Ah, I see. How does she do that?"
A figure moved silently across the threshold, but Emily refused to look up, focusing more and more on the nubbled crayon and the lines of hope's fuzzy, bright-eyed face. She winced when delicate, mud-caked fingers selected a glass vase from the window sill and began to pick the water clear of old flowers and floating leaves.

"In the water." She sniffled, unsure. Her ambiguous reply meant to protect both herself and the kindly Dr. Kyeteler, who remained oblivious to the freshly filled jar set down onto the table next to him. When, momentarily, it did appear to catch his eye, Emily abruptly grabbed a handful of dry watercolor paintbrushes and threw them in, enough to startle the doctor as the old paint began to form purplish clouds on the bottom of the rainbow glass.

"Like that." She stated, pointing to the swirls of grey, green, and orange. "You make it dirty. So you can't see through it anymore."

Dr. Kyeteler straightened, knowing for a fact that there had not been a vase of water on the table when they sat down. Emily hadn't requested any paints, and it was utterly strange that the object in question had appeared there now with whirling shapes and faces suspended momentarily in time.

"That's the problem, right?" She continued, oddly metaphorical for her age. "It won't ever be clean again. You have to throw it away. So, what's the point?"

"But, Emily, it's not about that." He answered. "You know, everyone always asks the same question you're really asking. Deep down, how do they move on? How do they live with the horrible things that happen to them? How do they go on knowing there is more pain still to come? It's how they get stuck inside the fear and lose their ability to fight. But what they don't see is that what they're really trapped in is the present, in the middle of the cloudy water before it settles. That pain isn't in the future. It isn't even in the past. It's just here, right now. That's why some people hurt themselves or they hurt others. And every time someone gives advice, like, 'find something to look forward to' or 'you'll learn to make it a part of you,' it fails for so many people. Because it's not about the future. It's about finding hope for the now. Right now. I mean...telling someone you'll turn the light on in the morning doesn't make the night any shorter."

Hannalore rose up from behind Emily's chair and ate the crayon.

SEVEN

With his usual smile, Armin Kyeteler opened up what he didn't know would be his last session with Emily Pendleton on the back of a pointless question.

"How are you today, Emily?"

He hadn't seen her in nearly three weeks, and she looked haggard but somehow content in her mild and gentle expression, tapping her shoes on the floor in an energetic rhythm. His notes, however, still traced the outlines of his increasing concerns.

He had written copiously about her continued references to ponds and bowls and the endless succession of goldfish that inhabited them as the only real sense of time she had anymore. And about Hannalore, the ubiquitous presence that both framed and calmed her fears, that he had long diagnosed as a child's mental trick to externalize the pain of neglect and to reach out to the remote parts of herself that hurt the most. What he wasn't expecting was the fact that Emily had come to this afternoon's session, in a word, prepared. She was holding a plastic bag filled with water in her lap.

"I'm good."

"For a moment there, I thought you had brought your fish along with you today. But no? I don't see anything in the bag."

"It's for just in case." Emily replied.

"Well, now you know I'm going to ask you, in case what?"

"In case you can't keep it."

At the end of their meeting before this one, Dr. Kyeteler had pressed Emily on two particular fronts. The first, on whether or not any of the goldfish she described had ever actually been alive and the second, on what it would mean to 'see' her friend. At which point, quite unexpectedly, Emily had offered to introduce him to Hannalore. Face to face, on the couch, the next time they spoke. But her offer had also come with a rather funny warning; he had to be sure he had the time to devote himself to a new pet.

As a result, the psychologist had thought it virtually guaranteed that his patient would appear in his waiting room with her mother and a fish. Instead, he now pondered the meanings behind her arrival with her father — unwashed, disgruntled, and silent — and an empty bag of water. She was also now sitting to the furthest right side of the couch across from the therapist, as though attempting to center his attention on someone else who had yet to make themselves known.

"Alright then." He continued in his typically affable manner. "I'll follow your lead. How does this work?"

Emily squeezed the bag as she chewed on her lip. Glancing to her side, she wasn't quite certain what to say, given that her friend had arrived so impressively dressed for the occasion.

When the uncanny wished to celebrate, she thought, they certainly did so without such formalities as shy delegation or timidity. Today, layers of decomposed fabric clung to the still form in twists shaped to look like reverberating surface waves, making Hannalore's stiff posture all the more like a forgotten stem enshrouded in wilting petals long faded from red to brown to grey.

The strands of her hair were equally tended so that the long locks fell around her face and eventually threaded into the stitching to form the embroidery. There, her own skin and mane completed the presentation such that it was impossible to tell the difference between what she wore and what she was.

"Well." Emily finally replied. "The first thing you have to do is answer some questions."

"Ok. What's your question?"

She squirmed and looked back up to her friend, who only stared straight ahead with a wan smile and unmoving eyes. "Not my question." The girl muttered, fixing her gaze back onto the reflections in the water she held. But he did not hear her.

She took a deep breath. "Why do I have to come here if you know you can't help me?"

Kyeteler was taken aback and slowly laid his notepad aside. "Emily, what are you talking about?"

"Why do you say I have to come back if you can't help me?"

"Do you really think I can't help you?"

"You can't ask me questions right now. I ask you the questions."

"Ok. But Em…"

"No."

"I…ok. Let's see." He was pensive now, growing worried. "I would say that I want to see you as often as I can because I do think I can help you."

"You can't." She sniffed, partly angry and overwhelmingly sad. "You can't change what's happening. You can't do anything about it. You can only tell me to feel things I don't."

"Emily, if something is going on, if someone is…"

"Why do you pretend that what you do changes anything?"

Why he answered the way he did, Armin Kyeteler would never know, but his words were reflexive, almost mechanical. "When I was a kid, someone once hurt me too. I know what it's like, I really do. And when I meet other kids who've had the same experiences, I know I can show them a way through it because that same pain is here with me."

Emily scowled and looked away.

Dr. Kyeteler suddenly froze, his eyes shifting left and across the empty space that had, only moments before, held nothing. It still held nothing but now he was less sure of it. Nothing moved or had a shape like shadows in a hallway.

Nothing brought back the voices from downstairs whose muffled screams blended with wind, creaking sideboards, and the crack of a shattering vase thrown against the wall. It watched him with vacant eyes and spoke with an open, blackened mouth.

Nothing at all but the horrors he couldn't stop seeing inside himself and in unfilled, unoccupied places. It was grey, he thought, or maybe it wasn't a real color at all. He turned back to the girl on the couch.

"I don't think this is a good topic of discussion." He stated. Fear crawled up his neck.

"You have to answer the question." She repeated. "You have to. If you want to see."

"I...I told you. I've been there myself."

"But you're still there though, aren't you? If you're still there, how can you lead anyone out of anything? You're just here, right now, like me."

"Yes, I'm...I'm here..."

The left-most shadow moved again, and the psychologist couldn't help but follow it. A figure rose up from the cushion and seemed to loom over him.

He could feel the weight of it as it raised one foot and then stepped up into his lap, pointed toes digging in to his thigh for purchase. Tangled bones knitted into the visage of a woman as three crumpled fingers unfolded to caress his cheek.

"What...what is this? Em...Emily?!"

"It's ok." The small voice receding into the background assured. "You can meet Hannalore now. Just like you wanted."

He did see her then.

He did see what wasn't there.

And when he screamed, the sound vanished into the void of an open hand and then an arm that took the invitation and slid down his throat until it grasped the breath he'd been holding since the day he had first tasted death and trapped it in a closed fist.

He stared up helplessly, his own arms useless and twitching, as the desiccated face that hovered over him tilted and blinked once. He tried to gasp but she had that too, and something like bile and slime quickly filled his mouth. When the thrashing started, he prayed for unconsciousness.

On the far end of the waiting room, however, Neil Pendleton had grown impatient, and the odd noise of a snapped-off cry had him striding towards the psychologist's door with an irritated sense of purpose. But before he could knock, or even just burst in as he might be tempted to do, his daughter emerged.

She pushed the door only so far as she needed to slip through and stepped out, closing it politely while waving to her father as she then trundled past.

"Hey!" He called out, motioning towards the office. "Everything ok?"

"Yeah." Emily said, without turning or stopping. "It's fine. He doesn't want to see me anymore though. So, we can go now."

"What? What do you mean he doesn't want to see you anymore? Em?"

When the girl paused long enough to acknowledge her father, Neil couldn't help but get a sense that something truly strange was going on. She looked brighter, happier in a way that he hadn't seen her, and without the dark stormfronts that had followed her everywhere the past few years.

Her pale, floral shirt and printed skirt even looked to have taken up more color in the interim between their argument at this morning's breakfast and now. Her cheeks were flushed but her hands shaky.

"Emily? Are you ok?"

She nodded.

"Where, uh...where's your bag of water?"

She smiled.

"Dr. Kyeteler decided to keep it."

EIGHT

"Hannalore? Will you tell me a story?"

"Yes, Button. What kind of story would you like?"

"I don't know. Something I can think about until I fall asleep?"

The late moonlight barely illuminated the parched, cotton-mouthed features of her friend, folded lengthwise across the end of her bed.

"Well, that always makes me think of the two men on the banks of the river." She began. "It's a story that starts just like any other. The kind where the story-teller says, 'one day there were two men walking along the edge of a river.' You picture them in whatever way is most meaningful to you and then they say, 'As the two men walked, discussing the events of their day, they happened to notice another man, floundering and floating away, trying to swim but failing and therefore drowning in the water.'"

Emily rolled over. "Then what happened?"

"They looked up along the current and to their horror, the men saw many people in the river. All getting washed down by the strength of the flow. People scattered everywhere, trying desperately to find their way back to the banks."

It seemed an odd kind of bedtime story, but Emily was already used to Hannalore's odd way of telling them.

Her friend continued. "So, the first man, without even a moment's hesitation, threw off his jacket and leapt into the river to begin pulling people out as fast as he could. One after the other, no matter how far it took him into deeper and more dangerous water. But then, after a time, he suddenly noticed that the other man was not in the river with him nor was he helping to pull the people out. When he looked around, he only saw his back, receding up the hill as the other man ran as fast as he could."

The little girl thought she understood but said nothing as Hannalore murmured the conclusion. "He called out to him. 'Why won't you help me? Where are you going?!' The other man only paused for moment to turn over his shoulder and call back."

When the resulting silence stretched on just a little too long, Emily prompted. "What did he say?"

"To stop whoever is throwing them in."

"Hmm. That's not much of a story."

"That depends. On whether or not you want to keep telling it."

Emily smiled and snuggled into her bedcovers. This had actually been Hannalore's habit for some time now: giving her the barebones of a tale only so that she could fill in all the interesting details herself and fall asleep while doing so. This, she undertook now. Why were there people in the river, who were the two men, how did they know each other, and, of course, what villain lay up ahead who could do such a thing as throw everyone he met into the dangerous water?

When Hannalore quietly rose and drifted ponderously out of the room, she was halfway to imagining a terrifying monster rampaging through a fairy-tale village in its quest for children to feed to the ever-hungry waters of a haunted stream that smelled of rancid breath and astringent, rotting wood. Emily did this because she had come to believe that the best way to conquer her nightmares was to hold them out in front of her and pick apart their mysteries before they ever even had a chance to sneak up on her and frighten her in the dark.

It was also, strangely, the quickest cure for her insomnia.

At last, when the entire household slept, Hannalore crept down to visit the one soul that still stirred in the kitchen. The one who adamantly refused to sleep.

Bathed in the sickly light of the fluorescent bulb over the sink, Neil Pendleton sat at the table, hunched over a glass of whiskey mixed with unidentifiable leavings from the back of the refrigerator. He didn't startle or even breathe when the spindly form wandered in from the hallway, nor did he flinch when it came to rest on the back of the chair opposite him.

Instead, he took another drink and wavered, feeling that same bilious sensation rising up in his throat again. He tried to swallow it along with his chaser, but it stayed fixed. He still didn't look up and without warning, he sobbed out loud.

"I could have hit her." He choked, barely raising his bloodshot eyes.

"I know."

"Gets a mouth on her, you know. She needs to be...to be...knocked down a peg. Girls shouldn't talk like that."

Nails scraping across the thin laminate made him cringe away. "I mean, I can do better. I know I will. I just...I just have to, I mean, get her to understand that. My dad would never have allowed..."

Neil stopped to breathe, something at the back of his throat making the words harder to get out.

The empty glass was pulled away from his hand and taken to the dripping faucet by crooked shadows. As it filled with tap water, he stared angrily in the direction of his tormentor's indistinct presence.

"Don't make me do this again." He grated through clenched teeth. "Why are you making me do this?"

"I haven't made you do anything, Neil. I have told you this. If you cannot follow the rules, you must accept the consequences. Is that not what you yourself have said?"

Echoes reverberated outwards in his memories as the words skipped like stones across the surface. Had he said these exact things to his family? Was it something his own parents had said to him? He couldn't recall if there was a difference. It moved in his mouth, and he heaved, pounding an angry fist on either side of the cup set down below him.

"I said I wouldn't hurt her anymore."

"I know."

"You don't believe me."

"What I believe is irrelevant."

"You don't care."

"Of course I care, Neil. To leave such golden creatures writhing, dying, in a container too small to hold them without cracking is the greatest abuse one could conceive of. Lined up on the street corner beneath candied lights as they sink away to nothing. Huddled against the back walls of isolated rooms to live and die alone. What beautiful colors lie beneath drab and foolish faces, begging to be seen if only for a moment. What depravity to ignore them, to dismiss them, only because they are common."

With a pained groan, he retched, grabbing the glass as he tasted algae and felt the scrape of scales against his tongue. He struggled for air as his eyes went unfocused.

He could see nothing but meaningless grey patterns interspersed with the flashes of light his mind conjured with every convulsion of pain. The whiskey with lime made him slow, but the wounds in his soul, bleeding out, made him indignant.
"I don't understand. Why is this happening? ...Why...Why are you here? Why is it always you?"

"Well, I suppose I simply adore goldfish."

MEDITATING ON AN EMPTY ROOM

My self sits broken,
in a room devoid.
Four empty walls, a width of floor,
Stripped of thought, destroyed.

No footprints, no soil,
no reminiscent strains.
All that will be there, exists.
All that once was there remains.

My voice thus will echo,
As bone or birth ordains.
A wilted body, I become
Nothing.
And all that it contains.

I don't know what I was thinking when I promised to write a classic detective story. Even my editor seemed surprised. But the suggestion just came right out of my mouth before I'd even had the chance to catch up to myself on the street. Shouldering groceries and my phone, I justified it, to no objection, that everyone likes detective noir. It's iconic. And it's just about that time in every other decade since the 1930s that the genre gets a reboot. Which means that someone needs to get on with re-inventing it again.

Why not me? After all, who better than authors to find themselves trapped in the same recurring cycles of a hundred years, writing passé fiction well after the revolution of the last era and calling it avant-garde. But before then, I remembered that I had also promised to write a new edited volume of academic chapters; something where my colleagues and I each read an abridged version of the Bhagavad Gita and then give our individual interpretations regarding the omitted passages.

Unfortunately, I can't really tell the difference between peer review and line edits anymore and I'm always a little startled by what comes back after I've finished the latest submission. Because when it finally turns up again, it doesn't seem like it's really my work anymore. Think of a page in the Mahabharata covered in red notes inspired by Shakespeare, as if I'd had some random idea for a Sanskrit poem but someone else had revised it into Elizabethan English. I laughed. My reality is my fiction, and my fiction is that I am still a respectable scholar with a pleasurable pastime in writing novels.

On the other hand, haven't anthropologists always said that novels and monographs really aren't all that different from one another? Each one sets a scene, with a madcap cast of dramatis personae, and then tells us something about the world; a partial truth that is both fractional and contextual but still honest enough to mean something. A truth that must be interpreted through the time and place of its own making to get at the elusive substance beneath. So, in that way, does it matter how long I have been a fictional ethnographer? If I sent the wrong manuscript to the wrong publisher, would anyone even notice?

A day later, I sat pensively at my desk, twirling a pen in one hand. I even have half a mind now to replace it with a feathery quill. Some might call it pretentiousness, but I just can't seem to send my words out into the digital ether before I've had a chance to physically pull them from the chaos first. I need to hold them in my hands before they dissolve back into the eternal oneness of all existence again, and therefore, a fancy writing instrument is vital to the offerings I must make to summon them. The bad news though, is that today's prasadam is going to be my retractable Pilot rollerball in fading blue.

That's the worst part, I think. For all the years that I have been writing; staring out of the same, small, dirty window of my upstairs office, I've tried to pretend that there is a difference between a world and the world. That one of those worlds is authentic and the other a fabrication. No, that's not quite right. That only one is substantive while the other is certain. Wait, that's still not what I mean. That one is...legitimate? I'm clearly going the wrong direction here.

But where is the line between them; between the miniature diorama racing around outside my window and the mirror image of it that I can't ever seem to slow down in my head? And how do I get the people in my life, and the people in my thoughts, to respect the distinction? All I've wanted for so long now was to see them separate, or at least to glimpse it, in the stories constantly narrated by the voice scraping its bottom teeth across the inside of my skull.

It's no use. I have no other option but to be guided into the story. So, I begin the opening paragraph with an annoyed flourish:

The night will not go quietly. Digging its claws into the asphalt, deep grooves of storm-drained thunder form rivers of streaking stars into the sewer grate as the inevitable dawn hauls its unwilling hostage towards the horizon. The weak protests of a '38 Dodge Coupe barely test the midnight silence as the city desperately clings to what little is left of its last oath of secrecy.

There, a proper noir! Excellent. Now, to introduce my investigator, my voice of morality. I will have my structure done just right, even if I have to force it. And here I pause for far too long. He isn't coming together as he should. Where is the shadowy figure ready to challenge my claims to inspiration? Ah, then I see him as the car hesitantly rounds the next corner.

Krishna leans, shoulders squared, against the tilted lamppost, the lone vigilant guardian of a bright oasis in a desert of glass ice and frozen steel. He takes a slow breath from his last cigarette, counting the hours with the passing of sidewalk heels and weary engines. The deft Nizam flute graces his lips before being passed off in relaxed fingers to rest on a bended arm; notes of contraband Pune Blues drifting out in tendrils of smoke while the last remnants of a late-night song fall off the end to ash in the chill wind.

The dark fedora sits low, his eyes lost in the shadow-play from brow to knowing smile. A fine pose, knee bent, and posture curved, topped by a single peacock feather carefully poised in a hatband sanded smooth by rain and wind. Its third-eye glistens, blue and green; the coyly mocking witness no judge could hold in contempt.

Wait, which manuscript is this again? I stare blankly at my own letter-filled page. My mind returns to Double Indemnity, but my heart hears the shlokas of the eighteenth chapter, the Mokṣa SanyŌs Yog, where Krishna, himself a deity in disguise, counsels his friend Arjuna on the cosmic orders of duty, harmony, and death.

The Coupe's brakes grind ominously as it weighs anchor curbside, its tell-tale scrapes and marks testifying to a last run-in with the gangster's gun. The single detective at its helm casts a scowl before stepping free and crossing the dimming headlights, out of one revealing light and into another.

"If I didn't know you better, I'd say you were asking for trouble." He says.

"It comes around asking for me often enough. This is just a return on the favor."

All at once, my meditation takes hold. I realize that it doesn't matter what I am writing because I am writing it all. One text, one page for every ending. It doesn't matter who it's for; it's for everyone and anyone and me. Arjuna is filled with doubt at using his martial skills to kill just as much as I am seeking to slay my own disbelief and scratch my way through the long dark night of the soul and into darśan. He is reluctant to act because his enemies are his own relatives, beloved friends, and revered teachers. A feeling I also know all too well because my enemies are the same. So, he turns to his charioteer and guide, Krishna, for advice.

With a tense laugh, the other detective throws the car keys in a glittering arc, the chime of worn metal cut off by Krishna's quick receiving hand.

"We're due in Kurukshetra by sun-up. Best get a move on it." He says plainly.

"When kin and cousins do shady deeds, they don't palm their cards until all the bets are in. Didn't think you were out to deal until the ante's up." Krishna replies.

"Full house or pair doesn't mean much to the Kauravas bullet in your pocket and out your back. Ask any dead man about who gave him the head start, and he'll say he scored it from that guy, paid by so-and-so, working time with they and them. Five or six degrees and the list always ends with a show of hands sharing the same name. Time to draw the bow and forget the apple."

"Maybe, but a wall at your back doesn't guarantee the knife won't find it and you're not one to take aim before the funeral procession comes calling on its own."

Arjuna turns back toward the car, reaching for the passenger side door before meeting Krishna's curious gaze across the roof, trying to wring the pale worry from his face.

"Not this time. You've got the map?"

"Don't need it. Not the first time or the last time I've seen this fateful tale to its end. I'll show you how we get there."

I feel almost triumphant. Krishna has counselled Arjuna, my perfect anti-hero protagonist, to pay heed to the greater power of dharma once again, on these cheap notebook pages, just as he did in ancient calligraphy and trade paperbacks over the past millennia. Just as he has again and again in the arguments of theologians and in the dialogue of stage plays or movies, spoken by actors with characters carrying his face and called by his name.

He tells both us and Arjuna that death would involve only the shedding of the body and that the soul is permanent. Arjuna's hesitation, he explains, is merely his lack of understanding of the true nature of things. His fear and hesitation are thus the only impediments to the proper motion in the cosmic turning of the universe. Krishna has warned him, however, that without action, the truth will be forever obscured.

Yes, I too must act and then uncover that truth! I wave the pages over my head and the fish in their tank near my elbow scatter in a panic. This will be it. This will be the book I always imagined I could write after years, no, decades, of struggling through endless articles and reviews. How many glowering looks had I already endured or lukewarm opinion pieces that never seemed to get out of any of my words what I had put into them?

Clutched in my fingers was finally the novel that would change the world! A world for the world. No more toiling away in obscurity (if for no other reason than obscurity doesn't seem to pay very well) or endless sleepless nights cramped behind a pasteboard desk next to the fish tank! I've got it this time or, perhaps, it's just that the eighth time is the actual charm.

Shaking, I send the first chapter to my editor.

Three days later, she sends me a rejection letter with my name misspelled.

The loneliness creeps back in from under the front door. There are plenty of familiar voices on the other side of it of course, but I can't bear the thought of listening to the same scoldings they too will repeat forever. In that dark seclusion, I can't even look at the pages for another week. But then I keep seeing the corner of the top sheet jumping up into the breeze whenever I pass by.

It's beckoning me back to the desk, but I tell myself that it's just because the tip of my pen pressed so hard into the lines that the paper is now irrevocably warped. The damage I've done to the pristine sheet is what makes it act like that, and it's nothing more than the painful wince of a bruised handprint. It keeps happening, though, and eventually I can't help but read, and re-read, the words I've left out in plain view. Over and over, I repeat them.

It's at the point where Krishna and Arjuna are conversing. They sit side by side in the car, ambling through the rain like the suspicious archetypes of power, violence, sex, and death I'm supposed to be making some kind of commentary about. Stupidly, I realize what I've been missing! No noir could ever be complete without the dreaded femme fatale. It's part of the form and the function, and she's missing entirely! My antagonist, the very fulcrum by which the plot is set into motion, has yet to even appear. I've been absent and foolish. So, I flip to the next blank page, tear it out to stuff the mangled edges into the beginning of my notebook, and start immediately on the scene that must have come long before this one. Krishna's low, silken voice is all I can blessedly hear.

The first time I saw her, she was sitting in the rickety, hardback chair propped up against the door to my office. Not the better one, with the angled arms, on the other side of the desk, where new clients gravitate while in the slow orbit of a lifetime of debts. She also didn't look at me like they do, all confused desperation with pleading lips they hope I can read. No, not her. Radha was order and chaos wrapped in a Banarasi sari, etching an hourglass figure right into the varnish with a gold jaali lattice that rewrote the world into repeating patterns of knots and schemes.

Even her smile was a warning. Letting me know that the blues and greys from her shoes to her kohl-rimmed eyes were a decision made to match what she saw in me and the wool three-piece suit I was only obliged to wear on Sundays.

"The name on the door says Madhava." She breathed out the words by rolling her tongue against the back of her teeth. "But for a name like honey I'd have expected something sweeter than a man who looks like he could have spent the night passed out in the old man's cow pasture."

"And yet, you knocked."

"I'm looking for trouble."

"I'd say that's precisely what you've got already," I replied. "What you're looking for is a reason. Some cause and commentary, or maybe a confession, but I think it's less that I was what you intended to find and more like I just happened to be here when you arrived."

In my mind, Radha moved like the head of a great serpent, unnaturally steady on a sinuous spine that could turn whichever way she willed it to without so much as a twinge in her inflection. But this wasn't just about some metaphor for the venomous strike of a lurking cobra, it was about the choreographed steps in an infinite dance she lived to perform.

"Well, I certainly wasn't expecting the Vrindavan type, but now I'd say that Vrindavan doesn't strike me as the type for you."

I smiled in return. "Not to worry. Next time I'll come to work in a crown and garland and play the king. Give everyone the show they expect for as long as the stage curtains can stay up."

"I don't think it would help." She answered, hand to the arc of her hip. "Men like you might have a taste for a full audience and a crowded dance card, but I'm afraid that today, it's just me. That why I've always hated poker, you see? A full house should never beat two of kind."

"No wonder you've got a thing for suits then."

"I think you've got me wrong, Mr. Kanhaiya." She countered, then touching her knee with the tips of her well-shaped nails. "I'm here about a case, and the word going around in my club is that you're the man for mysteries."

"Indeed I am. Which brings me to the fact that, right now, you're the enigma in the room. Or does that riddle come with a forward solution? What do they call you?"

"They call me with a need for answers." Her neck twisted as a vine in the tall grasses. "Their mouths water with daydreams where they see the flowers in my hair crushed and my braid pulled apart. Maybe even try to divine some truth in the scratch marks on my thighs. Desperate to know everything about me except for me. So, you can call me Radha."

She really had a way of answering questions, I had to give her that. She'd follow my lead, but only so long as it took for the music to change key and for the steps to reverse. I tipped my hat to her and offered to shake her hand. It seemed that our dance was about to begin.

I stopped and set down my pen. The line of photos on my desk, all in that same black and grey scale of the old cameras, looked back at me disapprovingly. The first one was of my mother, and her family, on the day she married my father. The one before that was my grandmother, and it was her wedding day, too. Then, my aunt and her sister, one beaming and the other scowling, on the respective eves of their matrimonies as well.

All my photos arranged neatly into a window pattern as panes of glass that looked in on my family's life from open mandir doors through the years. Amma, with her pallu tucked up and her hair tightly braided. My mother standing straight and tense with her hands folded at her waist. Followed by the empty space of undisturbed dust where my link in the chain of metal frames was supposed to have gone. And then, at the end of the line, the one burst of color in the whole tether.

I stared at the small brass statue on the edge of my desk, the Radha-Krishna my father had packed in my carry-on the day I left home for college. Krishna's sky-blue skin was matched only by Radha's white enamel with red tika and even redder lipstick. He was, of course, adorned in bright yellow with golden beads glued around the hem of his dhoti.

She was draped in a pink sari and a turquoise blouse, with layers of white garlands all the way to her knees. They both then shared a winding red dupatta; a long scarf meant to demonstrate their bond of eternal love as it wove in between their arms and around their shoulders. The perfect happy couple in their manacled joy.

It was such a quaint, familiar image, but all it did was make me feel ashamed. It might as well have been kitsch in a candy shop dispensing gumballs from the tops of their crowns. Press the painted toes and get a little laddu sweet for your troubles. Unfortunately, what I was supposed to do was look at it and see God.

But I couldn't see anything in it other than $49.99 on the internet and the chip in the base from where the bubble wrap hadn't entirely covered the stand during shipping. What was strange, though, was the shadow it cast onto my page: a looming, mountain-like shape with two sharp points that pricked the next blank line.

Arjuna tapped the edge of his boot against the base of the door and envied his charioteer, whose calm mien and sideways smile unnerved him. Passing beneath each rhythmic streetlamp flashed a fleeting moment of limelight that made the driver's seat a throne and each turn of the steering wheel a new twist in the Sudarshan chakra that heralded the circle of inevitable dharma. But the car hummed along, oblivious to the predetermined roads neither of them had any choice but to follow.

"If you're thinking of anyone else, don't. It's the fear making up those stories, and that's just payment on a debt you may not owe." Krishna sighed.

Arjuna didn't understand. "I guess this is just the first time I've had to kill someone I knew so well and liked so little. Bonds of blood are the obligations we're born with; the debts we incur for the skin and bones we're renting. Death is one hell of a receipt for making a wager on a bit of life."

"Is that what you see?" His companion replied, his eyes never leaving the path ahead. "Sin for sin, trading against greed for a handful of exact change and a charge of treachery? Unforgivable actions that sever the ties the universe imposes upon us for a mere moment, even though those ties are the very thing from which wickedness forms?"

"Destroy the family and destroy all morality." The latter detective growled, trying to lose himself in the soft din of the city. "Just watch. My own grandfather will take the gun from my hand. My guru will throw the bullets into the mud. My cousins will strip the badges from my chest and wear my hat in lieu of my head as trophy on the wall."

It was the even softer laugh, though, that drew him out.

"You grieve already, even before they are dead. Then you will grieve after, such that all your life is spent in mourning for the living, the dead, the not yet born, and those that never will be. But go back to your long stares out the window, Arjuna, and see that the rain falls from the sky, drains away into the gutter, and then soaks into the ground. You call it waste and therefore it is lost for all time. What you will not see then is when it returns to the sky to fall again, just as this rain has fallen before. You only grieve because it drips through your fingers every time you try to catch it, thinking it gone forever if it is not kept tightly in your palm."

I did not write this. I don't remember it, and yet the last divot on one of my signature a's was definitely coming from the pen in my hand. I thumbed through the disordered sheaves of notebook paper, trying to find where I had put the beginning. I must have accidentally shuffled the torn page to the back because that's where I found a new scene.

"I have enemies, you know." Radha drew her hand down her neck to pet the velvet trim at her waist. "Calls himself Mura. But sometimes, he goes by other names. You know how it is. These gangsters always do, right? There's nothing more treasured by the greedy than another name to spread their legend far and wide to every person who hasn't learned the first one. You know Kamsa, but I know Kali. I know their anger, you know their violence."

Krishna pulled a cigarette from the pack and set it aside, tipping his fedora towards the mystery in the Banarasi sari. "Then by your word, let them be forgotten."

"You can do that, can you?" Her raised eyebrow spoke all the other incredulous words her sensuous lips didn't bother with.

"The distance between us is no simple room in a dreary high-rise with a creaking chair and a broken lighter." He answered. "Yours is the riddle, so mine had better be the result. But I keep thinking it's more like a poem I once wrote, except it wasn't very good. If only I could remember it again, tell it like it is now so that someone out there gets it. Then, those enemies would have an adversary they couldn't beat. Fight the fight the whole world's been waiting for. After that, you and I? Well, then you and I hit the corner supper club, and we see just how much the tango has on a good Manipuri-style."

"Hmm. Sounds like you need a good patsy. Anyone in mind?"

"The hardest thing in the world is knowing how to know oneself. But this one is dignity distorted, bravery masking faults. He'll stand before a mirror, screaming at the man reflected in it because he can't tell that he's exchanging gazes with his own eyes. But when you see him, you can tell that his shadow is an extension of the truth."

"What's his name?"

"Arjuna Purusarsabha."

The notebook slipped from my fingers and exploded onto the floor, unbound pages with hastily torn edges sliding in every direction until half of the scrambled paragraphs had vanished under the furniture. The pages I had been reading, of course, went right into the fish tank.

"Well, that's just...as well."

But with the words scattered every which way, it meant that I was alone again. Sinking down into my chair, with the single bulb flickering over my head, as God and my relatives all stared back in judgement. I suppose they had caught me, mehndi red-handed. So, I nodded and guiltily gathered up my blasphemy until it formed a curled, soggy lump I was obliged to keep in the metal trashcan so that it wouldn't drip ink and pulp all over the desk.

This also meant that now, what remained of the notebook was plain and untouched. Made clean again by my failures. Repentance pricked at my eyes with double needles of shame while the sodden sound of a conch shell filled my ears with the roar of a raging army. It was not the first time in my life that I had veiled my face with my own tears. In fact, that's how all of the women in my family had observed their ghoonghat. By making nods to propriety with silent heartbreak and beads of grief. I picked up my pen to fail again.

Arjuna stood as far back in the safety of the alley as decency would allow. But his vantage point still showed a line of Ford 18 V8s in that kind of matte black paint that made them perfect for an unseen getaway. On their hoods and in their windows, the muzzles of Thompsons and a few Sweethearts leaned out to catcall the rain for passing kisses.

Except for the one .38 Special cradled by an imposing behemoth of a man they all called Bhishma, but whom Arjuna had called daada. As he had been told from the start, every face that awaited him had a name he had known since before he could trust it. Uncles, teachers, brothers, and sons. Kinsmen, and every one of them there to rope him and dodge the heat.

"You don't know them, so I'll save you some time." Arjuna began. "Public Enemies All Numbered One."

"I know everyone," Krishna replied, bending the brim of his hat. "And I have more time than the world these days."

"Madhava, this can't be right. Maybe if I just go at it straight and break some deserving nose, we could walk from it. A bloody knuckle is nothing to losing every one of my senses and then still having to sleep at night. And sure, maybe that means I get a year or two before some second cousin to a third aunt blades me at the lunch counter, but I go out without an anchor to drag or an anchor dragging me off the bottom of the river."

Krishna smiled and tossed his head to brush a long black curl behind his ear. "You were always the one who had to make sure he wanted to know what he wanted to know. Still wish you wanted what you know?"

"That I take no pleasure here? That I know. But you say that we have a duty to destroy corruption, and I say that corruption is done in the destruction. No woman, nor daughter, nor son, who lives longer than this moment will ever see anyone but a midst of murderers. And I'm about to make them all right about me. No more brass cutting me favors in the card game, and as soon as the police get hot, they'll be sure not to deliver."

"You think nobody sees you, falling through every crack in every sidewalk path you try. Loving some job like it's all there is. As if eating up all their wealth and treasures would see even a single child fed. Or that strolling up with an unarmed fist is some kind of virtue that will finally pay off your mistakes because your brother will put a bullet through it to ruin your dice game just before he puts the second one through your heart."

Arjuna turned away, unable to face the other with his downcast frown. "You speak as if arrows are alms."

My hand stopped. The lines of the next verses flowed through my mind, but since they were not my words, I felt such embarrassment for even daring to think that I could write them down using my own chewed fingers. To do so would make them real before me.

They would exist in a way that my fractious brain alone couldn't accomplish. Their soul would acquire a body, youthful with freshly smeared ink but on old, brittle paper that was near to passing. And then, after that, I would have to write them down again. But would I do it the same or differently?

"Weapons can't cut." Krishna laid his hand on the withered shoulder of sorrow. "Fire can't burn, water can't make wet, and wind will not dry what is unfathomable and eternal. Because wounds, burns, drowning, and starving are things that can only happen to bodies. Those which we discard from our winning hand in the last round of play anyway. It is the same for both compassion and cowardice, neither of which will be coming by to show you around."

"So, you're saying that I don't matter."

"I'm saying that what matters is not I."

"And yet, I am awake when everyone else is asleep, and asleep when everyone else is awake."

"That's because it is night for everyone but us. You and me? We don't care how we die or where we fall because we're already there, and we'll be right back to where we started before anyone knows it. Or, at least, I will be. You just be sure you make it on time, or you'll be stuck in that same cell with no door and a useless lock. I'm not busting you out again."

"But you'll be waiting for me whichever way the judge's gavel swings?"

"I won't even scuff the hubcaps pulling up to the jailhouse."

Arjuna reached up and took the hand at his arm into his own. "Then, at least there will be peace for all those who live in the upstairs and the downstairs. Tenements losing their bricks to the storms in their mortar but no longer whittled down by every stray shot that happens to wander by in a day. Peace in this small part of the city at last, or for as long as it's our time. Kids will be back to stickball in the street, and the old lady up on 7 will lean out onto the sill to look for the milkman on his usual route. Families on an afternoon trip to the park with their strollers won't think twice about left or right. If that's all I can do in this life, I think I can live with that. You in?"

The laugh that bolstered him was gentle and genuine. "We're all in."

"Alright, whattya say we shake a leg, clean this place up once and for all, and then maybe you can finally introduce me to that dame of yours?"

"I don't have a dame."

"Ha! I've seen you with her. Quite the item around town, from what I hear. You've got a dame."

"You know me better than that. I'm not in the habit of keeping on with some dish you'd have to put away and protect. Don't be confused by conflicting opinions or hair-trigger doctrines. Radha just likes a man who knows what he's drinking and forgets everything else when he's supposed to. It's love on her terms and idolatry on mine. So, keep steady, check the Gandiva's bolt and clip, and get in the back seat."

"You driving?"

"With six horses, twelve volts, and right off the edge of the world."

Slowly, I looked up from my stained palms and pages to the smiling photos I could suddenly see so clearly. Not judging me but gathering around my notebook to look at what I was writing and to be as much a part of it as I was. Cheering me on and celebrating in all the ways they had been told were improper. And there still were the murti of Krishna and Radha, a light green patina on the brass details, but completely resplendent in a new suit with a felt Cotswolder hat and a new sari of grey-checkered Kota Doria.

At last, I was dancing, my ras lila circle spiraling in around me. I felt the sob in my chest as I saw Them join us.

Radha sidled up to the bar and took note of the empty space before him, worn into a smooth, unvarnished circle by decades of slick glasses passed back and forth between anxious men with sharp insults. But instead of his next drink, Krishna rolled a small envelope in his hand, crumpled but sealed, as he considered whether or not he would open it.

"What's that for?" she asked, eyebrow raised in mild concern. "Time to take the next step on my behalf, or are you just here to listen to jazz and pretend you're a detective?"

"Why?" He chuckled. "You don't happen to play the sax, do you?"

"No." She smirked back. "But I hear you've got quite the talent with a flute."

"So I'm told." Krishna slid the unopened message back into his jacket. The next case would just have to wait a little bit longer. "But there are a thousand songs to play in a place like this and pretty much none of them are worth repeating a second time. I've made a better decision anyway. I'll be your agent, but you should know that I never kill for money and certainly not to get a woman. So, if you've got nothing else going on…"

"...you'd like to ask me for a dance?"

"I'd like to ask how it is that I have you when I never even had to get you?"

The laugh that followed chimed as bells across a snowy threshold, startling the bartender into thinking that a boisterous crowd had just now arrived. But it was only her and her flower-strewn tone, talking to the handsome man with the buttery skin and the fiery eyes.

"Well, we'll have to see about that then, won't we?" She replied. "How about you take my hand and start there."

With a nod and bow, Krishna stood and accepted. He stayed ahead of her but never turned his back, looking up at the passing crowd only once.

I could even have sworn that Krishna winked at me, an air of mischief in the rise of his chin. As if to say, "Nice to see you around again, doll. Been awhile. Turned into a real Gumshoe Gita though, didn't you? Well, it so happens that I've got a clue about that problem of yours I think you might want to hear. Cool your heels, lean in, and let me tell you about it."

Parlay?
— C

YOU'VE NEVER SEEN THE SUN

I am a traveler, who drifts,
I feel a call to walk the world.
An orchid grown crooked, burled.
Clouds pearled,
Shapes, shifts.

I sense the movement,
The flows that push my heels.
Until my path appears, reveals.
Compass freewheels,
Paused descent.

I cannot be but barefoot,
Even in verdant places boughed.
As the soil churns furrowed blood, plowed.
Cries for justice, avowed.
Raining soot.

It wells up through the dust,
Rising as a wave, it soaks my hems.
Seeping, seeping, through my stems.
I flower, condemned.
Petals rust.

The green is not grass but bile,
Poisoned life will spread, then depart.
Far away it will be barren, then restart.
I turn my back, falling apart.
One more exile.

NIGHT TERRORS AND NECESSARY EVILS

The goblins in the woods liked to take things. Trinkets at first, or just stray bits of trash caught up in the wind. But then they started coming further into the neighborhoods for more important treasures.

The first thing she noticed was when they took the voice in her head and replaced it with this one. Which might not have been all that bad if this voice, the one you're hearing now, wasn't so dull.

Unlike most kids her age, Cameo started using big words quite abruptly. As big as she could find them. Instead of saying 'try' she would say 'endeavor,' or instead of saying 'wonderful' or even 'marvelous,' she would say 'prodigious.' And instead of saying 'normal,' she would say 'that which is most trivially unextraordinary' in a tone of voice that well conveyed her constant discontent.

For a small girl not much more than twelve, with uninteresting hair and wire-rimmed glasses that left lines of acne across her cheeks, she made for quite the laughable figure in a small town with a small school. The resulting defensiveness then made her very unpopular. But while the word that usually came sailing right back at her was almost always 'snob,' she would brazenly inform her tormentors that she would settle for nothing less than 'erudite.'

None of this belied the fact, though, that no matter how many words she used, they were never big enough to be noticed. No matter how many her voice collected, no one seemed to remember what she had said. Too many letters and their meanings were weighted down, becoming too heavy to lift.

Too few and they floated away on the wind before anyone caught them. And so, the girl of twelve with the bent-wire glasses began to learn that the more she could say, the less those around her could hear. This prompted her to wonder if perhaps someone was taking her words before they could arrive at their intended destination. Or, if something was just outright stealing every annoyed glance that was supposed to be meant for her.

Then, the goblins appeared. They knocked politely and smiled when she answered. Now, no one would have thought there was anything out of the ordinary in this case if not for the fact that it was her bedroom door that opened to their inquiry and not the front gate.

The first one introduced himself as Versagen, and he seemed like a rather doubtful fellow. This was because his life-long propensity for failure had instilled within him a deep sense of inadequacy that tended to spread to the people around him. Which meant that he also had a habit of putting too much pressure on others to succeed where he had not. It then led to more errors and now even his own companions stood several steps away from him for fear that he would screw everything up before the greetings were through.

The second was called Ausgest, and he was a thief. Cameo didn't have to guess at this because he bluntly told her so. Though he assured her, his interests were very specific, and he had no use for expensive baubles, coins, or impressive price tags. The third and final visitor introduced herself as Forleer. Angry is how Cameo would describe her, no matter what she did. She stomped when she walked, shook her fists whenever she talked, and scowled even when happy.

She threw small objects off shelves as she passed by them and seemed like the type to bang pots temperamentally when cooking or to twist and fold cloth just hard enough that anyone in the vicinity would understand what it meant to have someone violently do laundry at them. Though, whether she was finding reasons to be mad or just to look like she was, didn't seem to matter. It was the same thing either way.

"So bona to varda your eek." The goblins said in unison. Apparently, they could only cobble-speak, using obscure words with meanings that were ambiguous or forgotten, since Cameo didn't understand the sentence at all other than to mean that they were pleased to see her. "May we make our way in?"

She stared at them, eye to eye and nose to nose. "What? In my room? No. Who are you?"

"May we have your name?"

She squinted past the small trio and into the hallway, but there was no one else there. She briefly wondered if this was some sort of prank. "What do you want?"

"Your name." All three said again, though not all at once this time.

"Why do you want it? I don't have to give you anything."

"Well," Versagen stated. "Technically, do. You who offered it up, actually. The crows have taken their cut of sounds already. Cut and gone. We're just here to collect the rest of it. It's all paid up, just like you said and said."

She continued to stare at them in disbelief. "Like I said?"

"Said and said." Ausgest cleared his throat and repeated the throw-away lines of an old argument in her own formerly chirped tone. "Why did you name me with such a stupid name? I hate it! You chose it, not me, and all anyone does is make fun of it. It's like you were naming a dog or something! Why can't I change it to something else? Give it back to Grandpa if you like it so much because I'm sick of paying for it. I'm done!"

"The dead and done-for are keen-keen on the barter," Forleer added. "Nanti dinarly. Good bargain."

"I...huh? Well...I'm not giving it to you."

"I see," Versagen answered with a pout, forming his words more carefully and directly in response. "Then we take your tongue, I dare. No sharda. Better your palare. No more words they could ignore then right? Everyone comes to listen to you when the silence get too too big. Make all hold on to everything you say. Bona, yes?"

With a shudder, she gave them her name instead. But it was all a ruse since she didn't like it anyway and already had another one. A much better one only the new voice in her head had spoken.

Each goblin bobbed once in succession and made a pact to see her again soon.

FEAR ITSELF

Patchling, Minnesota. A town conceived of and built among the winding streams on the margins of the Lake of the Woods by those who knew the Woods. It was both temporal and spiritual in every way that claimed a place within the Boundary Waters, yet still somehow avoided being thought of as just a fringe on the Iron Range.

A simple place, with little to recommend it, aside from a few picturesque homes on modest lanes, a grocery store with a bait shop, and a single ramshackle church in need of new fieldstone. The central doctrine of the most common Christianity was, however, utterly confused and neutralized by the everyday suffering of mundane lives.

There was the hardware store manager, who lost his daughter to a fever, setting up a tool shed at the edge of the cemetery and adorning gravestones with iron crosses at his own expense. Or the minister, long turned agnostic, who, despite meticulously caring for the altar and hymnals, could not bring himself to pray in public anymore and drank his afternoons away at the bar nearest to the back door of the nave.

Then the check-out clerk who also sold hand-made talismans to ward off the Evil Eye alongside witches' tally sticks and Tarot cards displayed with the same reverence as hand-tied rosaries of teak and maple. And at the center of it all, the bronze statue of the town's founder. A figure so old and broken that no one even remembered his real name. So, they had simply left his tarnished image on its cracked granite pedestal, not cleaned of lichen for two generations at least. But, despite the local folklore, his twisted visage wasn't meant as a warning to passing tourists. Rather, someone would have repaired him years ago but for want of a suitable plaque and something to write on it.

For these reasons and many more, there was no better way to understand Patchling than as an ancient borough that had grown tired of its own people. It was possible, of course, that a greater chronicle had been recorded in the registers of the town hall, but it had decayed long ago, right next to the dried-up baptismal waters and a font filled with moss. It was the aforementioned priest that Cameo thought of most often though. They'd always been at odds, the two of them, all the way back to when her parents were still sending her to weekly Sunday School.

That is, until such an incident as the one that took place during Summer Bible Camp where she had brought her favorite vampire novel to read during his lecture, and he had publicly shamed her before throwing it into the fellowship fire. As it had burned, she'd levied a curse at him. If her words were fit only for the flames, then his would be forever lost in the smoke. Doomed, she snapped, to an eternity of passive disinterest. Indeed, she had even added, what could be more trivial than his last Sunday's sermon about a boy who had once opened a hymnal that used to rest on the organist's bookstand only to find flakes of Christmas pastry between its leaves, shut up in its pages for a hundred years with no one the wiser.

After that, it was the same everywhere in this lake village. Endlessly toiling away in fields already marked off to become cremation grounds before the next generation had even been born. If there was ever something that needed to be said, though, it needed to be said about the toll the last three decades had taken on the town because never had there been a more nondescript Midwestern statement on neglect than this one. Sadly, it hadn't always been the case.

Once, Patchling had been a valiant holdout for the canonization of bad taste, with its avocado damask, glazed lamps, and vile coloration; with popcorn ceilings and wall-to-toilet carpeting so banal that it only served to remind visitors why they found back-road traveling so annoyingly repetitive.

No sooner had they left town than they ceased to be able to conjure a clearly detailed memory of it, and in looking back on an endless cycle of picnics and parades, they found that they almost never remembered the specifics of shop windows or meals. Such mundanities just ceased to exist in the stories told about it all later. And now, as one particular Patchling pondered her options for the day, it became apparent why.

If 'brown' could be described as a mood, the whole place was in such a mood today. Dust-caked workmen in diners balanced wooden spoons on the edges of clay mugs, twirled knives, or tilted upon the hind legs of their chairs until their heads reached the wall. A paneled wall where the owner had pasted gratuitous advertisements for coffees, beers, whiskeys, and other amber drinks.

The gravel streets fared about as well, their margins residing firmly in the hands of professional dealers in wholesale misfortune. Sheriff's deputies, sons of auto mechanics, and insurance offices of the kind that might not steal your wallet outright but who would certainly steal the life you were living in order to wedge it into the rhythmic machinations of the town's horrible design.

Wretches at the height of their misery, a category of humanity stretching all the way back to Cain and every one of them slowly drained of every other local color except for an inoffensive beige. Brown was, therefore, proof of the cankered over-civilization that produced both aristocrats and peasants, crops and weeds. From dust, everything had emerged and was now impatient to be reduced to that same dust again.

For Cameo, who had no friends to hang out with over the summer anyway, the overgrown park near the river east of town was the perfect hideaway where, at the very least, the water could mix with the dirt and become mud. Malleable, workable, mud. There, she set down the battered plastic lunchbox — 'RALPH' scratched awkwardly into the handle in block lettering — and pulled out an odd assortment of trinkets.

A pair of pansies plucked from a crack in a parking lot where they had been staging a purple and gold rebellion against the paving of the world, and then a red-paper origami four-finger fortune-teller game dropped by a passing kindergartener. To this was added a rusted safety pin and a nicely formed skipping stone that she possessed only because it had failed at its one purpose in the human world. It hadn't managed to bounce across the surface of water even once.

"Ok." She said loudly, "I've got something to trade. I want to make a deal."

As it was now the appointed hour, before the mouth of the river opened wide enough to swallow the sun into its void beneath the ground, the goblins dutifully appeared from the underbrush to inspect the offer.

"May we have your attention, please?" Versagen motioned to a gap in the small collection.

"Yes," Cameo replied. "May I have the floor?"

"Yes is yes." Versagen agreed, and the trade was done. One attention given for another attention granted.

As the goblins gathered up the pansies, paper, pin, and stone, Cameo glanced at the rushing water, uncharacteristically distracted.

"Does anyone else ever come here?" She asked.

The trio shrugged. "Maybe in back time but not now. Water carries too much too far. Get lost here, and you would have to be found someplace else. Like the pictures on papers in the post office."

A starling chittered overhead. An ant got caught in her sock and required rescue. The leaves of the maple on the far side of the bank shook loudly in the wind until the large flat leaves seemed to be clapping in unearned applause.

"I need a moment." She blinked hard to adjust her glasses on her nose and turned back to all the creatures in her midst.

"Too rare, too expensive." Forleer snapped. "Won't find no market for that. No offers, no birds, and no one to trade in tik-tik-toc-tocs."

The goblins were right to be cynical, and Cameo couldn't fault them for it, at least, not outwardly. The town's hospitality was passing quickly enough. This would be true even if kindness and courtesy were only fragile masks that made life appear beautiful, and not the distorted expressions of a malcontented principality.

In its dark hunger, Patchling welcomed only those it deemed worthy of welcome: from pale farmer's sons coming to breathe the pastoral air with its medicinal alfalfa manure, to rank-and-file soldiers retired from the affairs of empire ready to tell stories of their glory days to listless grandchildren on screened-in porches. Pansies born in concrete and skipping stones that didn't skip, and all other goblins, could keep right on passing through.

Cameo looked down at her hands just as her face pinched into a scowl. The tips of her fingers were drained white and numb. The bruise on her elbow was grey. Boredom picked at the edges of her mind and threatened to make the breezy dandelion-fluff dance of the river-park another meaningless waste of an afternoon. She called it 'empty time,' with no point other than that it had to pass by her.

Empty time didn't even bother to acknowledge that she was in its way. She was being side-stepped by yet another day.

"But I need a moment." She restated with greater emphasis.

The goblins sighed, Versagen looking to Forleer for a response. She puffed up indignantly. "More than one? Just a second. Better scarper then. Run on those bijou lallies. Borrowed time is future's dime. You take it, and failure sends it back, the Crow comes snap it up once then twice."

Cameo smiled and nodded excessively, with only every third word making it through to her.

"One second then. Those borrowed futures take failure back. Comes up twice."

With a triumphant bounce, Cameo thanked the goblins once more, swatted at an unseen gnat, and gathered her lunch box to go. It didn't escape her at that point though, that the label on the plastic lid had torn and that the white handle had picked up so much more dirt that the letters scratched into it were obviously darker.

As if limned and deepened by the earth itself in some sort of malicious trick to remind her of what she intentionally wouldn't see. She rubbed at the word with the pad of her thumb, but as her hands were also dirty, it just made the name that much more discernible. Frustrated, Cameo looked up as a sudden decision overtook her impulses.

She turned around briefly to see if anyone was watching. When no one but a few large black birds could be seen in the trees and bushes on either side of her, she grinned with open glee.

And threw RALPH into the river.

THE SACKCLOTH SOLUTION

The following day was much worse. Cameo herself was a bit sickly, but her breakfast seemed to have lost its color, too. The blueberry muffins, which were normally as sweet as candy floss, were tasteless and speckled with black motes like ink stains in the bread. The toast and jam she tried afterward fared no better, and she couldn't help but remark to the appliances that they were really falling down on the job this morning.

She then tried some left-over cereal but only ended up throwing that across the floor as a troupe of cockroaches scurried out from under the box lid in an attempt to escape the mediocrity inside. She checked the fridge but found only more of the same limp and lifeless food slowly mummifying under the intermittent fluorescent lights. It was as if the kitchen had somehow been robbed of all the goodness that a hearth ought to be able to bake into its daily bread.

A cheerful knock at the back door startled her. When she opened it, she observed the three goblins had returned, lined up shoulder to shoulder on the welcome mat so that none of their collective feet were forced to touch the cement stoop.

"Parlay? Parli? Palare? May we have a word?" They all asked.

"Fine. Now give one back." She answered.

"Whatever."

"Hmm. I don't like that one. Anything better?"

"Obdurate."

"That'll do."

She liked that word and rolled it around on her tongue. It would be fun to use at dinner. Which was important, she informed herself, given that the food certainly wasn't going to be a highlight.

"We come to offer you a warning," Versagen announced, but Cameo couldn't help raising an incredulous eyebrow.

"What'll it cost me? You're definitely not here to give out anything for free, are you?"

The goblin frowned but did not dispute her insight. "May we request your assistance?"

She tapped her foot and sighed. "Have a good day, then."

Forleer accepted the trade and made good on the return. "Aunt Nell says a barney comes. No cackle. A right fight. Gonna break the eek and ends."

Cameo rolled her glasses up into the fold of skin at the top of her nose. "A fight? What for?"

"Luster."

She didn't understand and so looked for other words.

"Who's coming to quarrel?"

"Two violets too weak to find the break and a whirlybird, ripped up on the sand. And skipping stones took out of the river to put in the church foundation. Skipping stones took out of the river and stepped on to make a path that others walk."

Cameo was still unsure what all this meant, and it showed in the way she rocked back and forth on her feet. In the way that she glanced back and forth at minute things that blinked in and out of her vision or got caught on her lenses. In the way that she picked at her lip and chewed an uneven line across the chapped skin. She had already forgotten that she wanted to ask who this Aunt Nell was.

"Will you give me their names?"

Ausgest placed a hand on each of his companions to quiet them. "No keep." He growled. "Too many. Too mogue. We can screeve them to a scrap, but then you burn it 'fore any Crows come."

Cameo felt oddly pleased that her mind could easily translate everything he had said into strange sensations and misplaced twitches in her chin and elbow. Instead of fully comprehending his meaning, she felt it in her body. Somehow, she knew that five people were going to cause her trouble, and the goblins had written their names down on a bit of paper she'd thrown away somewhere and would have to be sure not to throw away again.

"Agreed. Not to keep. Just as long as I need them. Then I'll give them back. Might have to spell them different though." She said.

"It will be a steal, time for rhyme. What makes a word, makes a name, we get the inferred and you take the blame."

Cameo countered with her father's favorite scolding. "Blaming everyone but yourself means you don't have the power to change anything."

Forleer shook her fist, and the bargain was struck. On a slip of paper made from three bits and a gum wrapper taped together, the goblin had scrawled the names Justus, Deacon, Charity, Clem, and Grace.

Cameo took the note and stared at it. She knew the people the five first names were attached to, but why the goblins saw fit to choose these individuals in particular escaped her. She had, truthfully, expected a list of playground bullies.

Not a series of random peers who had done nothing but completely ignore her existence from birth to the seventh grade. To them, she was a passing phantom, and so, to her, they weren't much more than reflections in the background. Or now, letters on litter. With her damp thumb, she erased the names and handed the paper back.

With that, Versagen, Ausgest, and Forleer bowed and vanished.

Unfortunately, the clever girl did not fully realize the implications of exactly what the goblins had taken for the name trade until her family had disbanded after dinner. Her mother to the television and her father to the garage. Her older brother to his room and the cat to the all-consuming darkness of the back cornfield. Once more, left alone in the kitchen, Cameo finally began to notice a troubling forgetfulness.

Not the kind of forgetfulness of random details that usually comes along after an exhausting day but rather the kind where she could no longer remember what her favorite song was, what subject she was best at in school, or what side of the house her grandmother's irises grew on.

Though she tried, she also found that she couldn't remember what holiday came next in the year and observed that her memories of the best Christmas wrapping paper she'd ever seen were being replaced with the sounds of her elementary school teachers repeating the same four disciplinary slogans to her in tones that implied that she was too stupid to have learned them the first ten times.

Thankfully, the narrator in her head pulled her aside and snapped her to attention. One must oblige the reader, after all. And she had already lost more than she'd bargained for. She was giving too much and fading away.

HAVOC

Early the following morning, Cameo was nowhere to be seen at the breakfast table. She had left the hour before, pedaling her bike as fast as her short legs could go. She whizzed past the park, through the middle of town, and around the nameless founder, until she dumped the blue middle-wheeler, with its woven plastic handlebar basket, onto the lawn of the local library. From there, she had gone running in through the front door, heaved a breathless 'hello' to the surprised woman at the check-out desk, and then dashed into what served as the non-fiction section.

Small libraries such as this one did not have the privilege of expansive categorizing. There was simply not enough room in the old building to separate geography from astronomy or poetry from novels. And so, as was the case in the Maud Hart Lovelace Memorial Library of Patchling, Minnesota, books on every subject tended to be stacked alongside books on every other subject to create a mishmash of collective knowledge that would have had Carl Sagan reading Alice in Wonderland to Simone de Beauvoir while Friedrich Nietzsche laughed at Tolkien from the rafters.

It was exactly as Cameo wanted it to be, though. This library was her soul.

She tried to remain outwardly calm, but even unsugared at nine in the morning, her actions were frantic. She needed to fix the wounds and fill the gaps before she lost herself completely. Replace the missing memories and gather more words. She needed words to protect herself with and more words after that to replenish her bleeding spirit. She started with the first red book whose cover caught her eye.

It was an ornamental copy of Samuel Taylor Coleridge's Rime of the Ancient Mariner. Bound in crimson cloth and oversized to the point that the binding was half her height, Cameo could barely get the book upright before it flopped over onto its side and opened to a random page. She stared down at the first lines, instantly searing them permanently into her mind.

The many men, so beautiful!
And they all dead did lie:
And a thousand thousand slimy things
Lived on; and so did I.

With a grin, she set the massive tome aside, leapt up, and began to trace her fingers over the shelves for the next book she might feel a sudden and unusual kinship with. Her nail caught on the torn corner of a paperback that had once depicted a rearing horse and black-coated rider. She grabbed it and let it fall open to the page just after the broken crease along the back.

Expect nothing and fear nothing, here or anywhere. That's your first lesson.

Susan Cooper's The Dark Is Rising then joined the pile on the table. From there, an absolutely ruined copy of Stephen King's The Gunslinger added: The mystery of the universe is not time but size, and where the world ends is where you must begin.

Immediately following it, as her eyes darted left, she saw a book-plate dedication to one Charles Maurice de Talleyrand: Wherever there's trouble, look for a priest.

The quote wasn't meant kindly. But Cameo stopped to recite each line again to ensure that she was remembering them wholly and correctly. When she got to the last one for the third time, it occurred to her that there was still one more empty space. The piece torn out of her conscience remained ragged. She wandered out to the furthest shelf, the one from where she had not yet chosen any books.

It was a foreign language section that, much like the rest of the library, made no meaningful distinctions. Books from Japan sat beside books from Sweden, or even books from 18th century Russia and modern Russia, in no particular order. Once again, everything blurred together into a single perpetual present that could only be experienced as existing right now, all at once, in this one rural town.

Her hand stopped on a bright yellow jacket with loopy red writing. When she dropped it open to a page, the words came to her immediately and with such gravity that it stopped her cold.

Do not say, 'It is morning,' and dismiss it with a name of yesterday. See it for the first time as a newborn child that has no name.

Rabindranath Tagore was not a poet she had ever heard of, but she was sure of it now that he would not be forgotten for as long as she lived.

Momentarily reinforced with armor made of bookmarks and obsessive recitation, Cameo then checked out her prizes and loaded up the strange collection into the basket of her bike. As she made her escape on the rickety two-wheeled steed, she barely had to look up or look around to see what was truly happening to the sorry old patchwork town she had no fondness for at all. What goblins had taken from her; they had taken from everyone. The town was slowly being unstitched and had come apart into frayed tatters no one had noticed.

They just brushed it off their shoulders as a tuft of lint. But she could see the goblins now, stealing from everywhere. Draining the life out of everyone to hide it away beneath cedar chest lids and dusty shoeboxes in the backs of closets.

Keeping secrets in attic chests, or nooks filled with birthday presents hidden away too early so that they were never remembered even a generation later. But no one else seemed to see it as she did. They just shrugged and stared at her with angry eyes of regret and jealousy. The more color they lost, the more they clung to the beige spaces and empty time.

Goblins, as it turned out, had long found it to be true that before any vice could fasten itself onto a body, mind, or moral nature, it must be debilitated first. Patchlings were then especially procurable. Mosses and fungi gather, after all, only on sickly trees, not the thriving ones, and the odious parasites which are able to latch themselves onto the human frame tend to choose those which are already enfeebled.

Indeed, whenever the wandering demons of sin and malfeasance were to find a ship adrift, so to speak – no steady wind at its sails, no thoughtful navigator directing its course – they would instantly step aboard, take the helm, and steer it straight into the maelstrom.

This was why the Church so delighted the town with its proofs of purity; where healthy skin and whole flesh could be seen as evidence of Divine favor because no pestilence or corruption could stick to it and render it unclean. What, Cameo then wondered, might they say of her? Whose flawed complexion and unimpressive countenance had nothing to do with the abandonment of God but was simply the rent she paid on the erroneous body she was assigned.

She pedaled harder because she knew exactly where she needed to go. A minute later, the church was in sight. To fight goblins, she was going to need someone who could keep a Word. Someone who could follow the changes in its meaning but keep it all the same. Which was to say that there was, indeed, trouble. And she needed to look for a priest.

WHO CLEFT THE DEVIL'S FOOT?

Father Olson sat on the lone fold-out chair set up a few feet from the door to the nave, a coffee cup, smelling strongly of something other than coffee, clenched tightly in his fingers below a scowl blurred from two days' growth of peppered beard. What a poor wretch he presented, who had so readily sat down on the muddied cassock and threadbare stoles of his own reputation. The kind of man whom the papers still treated with an array of kaleidoscopic praises due to his station. Phrases which were carefully arranged in ever so many charming patterns, so as to be at the service of a saintly churchman tasked with the precarious salvation of bucolic souls.

But in rural backwaters like Patchling, smaller authorships were the provenance of truth and would note that such chips of tribute, fragrant and sappy, were the fictions of all men of the cloth. Chips meant to hide the peeling veneer of brittle prestige that this man now openly drowned in sour mash and a dash of brandy. Which is to say that he may have been ordained, but no one would have mistaken Father Olson for respected.

When Cameo saw him, however, she set her jaw, dropped her bike, scooped up the books, and marched straight over. This was, unbeknownst to many, an incredibly brave act. Father Olson had been nothing short of her personal nemesis since a Sunday School brawl last year had resulted in his discovery that she was changing into herself without his permission. As a minister, he'd apparently always seen himself as something of an authority on the transformation of souls, but this one hadn't so much as consulted him once on the matter.

Rather, she was embarking on a path of revelation that adhered to neither chapter nor verse. He'd taken it as an insult and called her a demon. Mischievous, ugly, and small, not to mention self-indulgent and base. Thus, she had gone out and remained among all the other goblins cast out of the church.

"Father Olson." She stated flatly, peering at him over the shield of Coleridge.

He stared back at her, confused. Cameo's family had never been particularly churchgoing, limiting most of their visits to Easter and Christmas, but ever since their last conflict, he hadn't seen any of them at all. Especially not her.

"What do you want..." He stopped suddenly. He realized, to his immediate concern, that he couldn't remember her name. He had been about to say something, but then an R and an L blended together on his tongue and caught in his throat. Try as he might, the name wouldn't come.

"It's Cameo right now." She replied before he'd even had the chance to sputter through the rest of his nonsensical sounds. "I'm using it until I'm old enough to get out of here. And just so we're clear, my real name isn't for you or anyone else in this town. I'm going to give that first time to someone really special."

The old preacher blinked, his face turning dour. "Fine. What do you want then, uh, Cameo?"

With strange aplomb, the girl hauled up her books and sat down next to him on a stone bench. "I need your help. Before I go, we have to save Patchling."

He almost laughed outright. She looked so utterly ridiculous, but her mannerisms were so incongruously confident. Her face didn't match her hands any more than her lime-green shirt could match her mustard shoes.

"Save the town? And what exactly seems to be the problem? Last I understood, you weren't a believer in repentance. Didn't even sign up for your catechism last year. Which, I should add, you'd be almost done with if you had."

With a deep sigh of annoyance, Cameo set her books onto her lap. "We don't need repentance, Father Olson. We need disruption. Disorder, disorientation, whatever it takes to break their hold. Don't you get it? I've asked the books and they told me everything."

"The books told you...everything? Cameo, there's only one book that..."

"Will you stop! Just for once and listen!"

He blinked again. Surely, he was in the presence of some imp come to collect on his many debts. No one spoke to him like this, not ever. He was hugged, and his hand was gripped with firm shakes of gratitude. He was told how good his sermons were and how nice it was to see him this week.

He was never challenged, never chastised, and certainly never disciplined by a twelve-year-old with a stack of library books. Still, he dutifully fell silent.

"It's the Goblins, and you know it! It's what they ask for and what they take. And every time they do, the world gets a little smaller. More ordered. More rules. More routine that can't be missed. Say the right things. Do the right things. Or face the consequences. That's how it's happening, and it's how it happened to you too, isn't it? It's all so safe and comfortable now, you think. All the bad things lurking just outside of our walls can't get to us because we built a fortress. But it was never out there, Father. It was always in here!"

"What are you talking about, child? Is this some kind of a joke?"

"No! It's not! Look, I've been thinking about this all day, but I couldn't figure it out. But then it just hit me! It's in the words! All the words that they stole!"

This was becoming absurd. "The words? I think you mean the Word..."

Again, she nearly shrieked. "No! You're not getting it. So close, and you're just not getting it!"

"Cameo, I'm serious. I don't have time for this foolishness today. If you want to have a real discussion about your faith, you know that I am always here to help you. But if all you're going to do is throw around some old poetry books or whatever this is, there isn't anything I can do for you."

"My faith? No, no, I don't think I have that anymore. I traded up on that already. You mean your faith. The one they took from you."

"What? What is that supposed to mean?"

Her smile at that moment changed everything. "Oh, now I get it. That's what happened. When they came to your door, they asked you THAT question, didn't they? That's what the Goblins came for when they came for you."

"Q-question? What question?"

She stood up, setting the books aside. She squared her shoulders and buckled her knees, standing in the same manner as Versagen. She even roughed up her voice to make it sound more like Ausgest with the quick, sharp gestures of Forleer.

"Father, may we have your blessing?"

GRIM AND PROPER

Father Olson wandered into the church proper as he slowly trailed after the odd girl, who was now inspecting the pews by picking up the hymnals, rifling through them, and then setting them on the seats.

"What did you mean by that question?" He asked, his head swimming with an unexpected sense of déjà vu.

Cameo looked up from a handful of Bibles. "Every time my dad took us all to one of your services, he always said the same thing afterward. 'You know what, kid?' He'd say. 'People talk like church and God are the most important things in their lives, but every person in that building this morning was just there so they could leave. Feels like all we were doing was waiting for an hour. 'Even Father Olsen?' I said. 'Especially Father Olson.'"

Glowering at the older man from over the tops of her glasses as she imitated her father's booming voice through the last line, she then dumped a large heap of various texts onto the platform leading to the pulpit. "And back then, I used to think it was because God had so many rules, and so many punishments if you didn't follow them, that people were scared. From the moment they stepped over the entryway, they called it reverence, but that was a lie. They were just scared."

Olson huffed and crossed his arms. "The church is a sacred space, Cameo. It is a place where the rules are different because we are in communion with the Lord."

Cameo shook her head. "Nobody talks to God here anymore, Father. They just talk to themselves. Or if they hate having to talk to themselves, then they talk to you."

Slowly, he looked about the church and took it all in, momentarily ignoring the shuffling and thumping he heard from pew to pew. This altar, with its outdated red carpet and wood-panel fronting, had been the same since he had first felt the Call.

A feeling, he realized, he couldn't seem to find right then. The large cross near the baptismal font was made of cherry wood, though, and the railing that closed off the front steps to make the communion knee-benches was varnished in maple. Nothing really matched, but it had a sort of charm to it, he thought, even if it was on the bland side.

He's always reminded himself that the interior decorating wasn't the point, though, and so whether or not the lectern and the crucifix clashed didn't matter so long as sacraments were done right. But when a strange sadness started to overtake him, he found himself blinking back a few unfair tears. It was so empty. And he only came here when he had to because he hated how lonely it felt.

"But!" He heard Cameo exclaiming. "Now we understand why."

"We...we do?"

"Yes! The Goblins." She stood up from the far end of the ambulatory. "Whatever they asked for, you gave them. Until everything was cut to pieces, and everyone had to follow new rules. Rules they didn't make, they just knew they should do. And didn't dare not. But the emptiness only grew. May we come in? May we have your thoughts on this...? May we have just a moment of your time? A prayer for us? May we take communion? Will you send us good wishes? Why do you believe this; give us your reasons."

"And so now you think that you...you...are the answer?" He sounded incredulous, but, in truth, Father Olson was becoming intensely curious as to what Cameo might say next.

"More." Was what she actually did say. "More words. We have to fill the empty time they've been making. Wipe clear the brown spaces they've covered over. Replace what they've taken with something new. New words, new music, new colors where they've hidden the old ones."

"Now, you just wait a minute." The preacher growled. "I don't care how much you see on the internet; there will be no new age services here, or whatever they're called. Rock bands and screaming into cameras, like those megachurches. We'll not betray who we are here. This is still a sacred place! A community!"

Cameo finally abandoned her trail of books and papers and pamphlets to walk over and look up at the man, flushed with fists clenched.

"Yeah." She said. "That's what I mean. Look at these empty pews, Father. Right now, no one who sits in them on Sunday morning is thinking about this place right now. They don't think about you, or the Bible, or the altar, or your words before they get here, and they don't think about them again after they leave. Most of the time, they don't even think about them when they are sitting here hearing you talk. But I now I see why."

With an almost imperceptible tremble to his lip, the broken man whispered his final benediction. "Why?"

"Because it's hollow. They left the grammar, you know, like all the rules, but took the meaning. So, fill this room, Father. And I don't mean with just Bibles and hymnals. I mean, with all kinds of words. Books of poetry, reflections, and stories. They need to have questions and answers of all different sorts. Meditations that affirm their love, and angry rejections that make them sad. Oh! And, and blank notebooks where they write down their own thoughts and feelings at the same time. They can take them home, write more about their experiences, and then come back next week and read them to each other. Read them to you! Then, people will become a part of a community, an exchange, where they will read and write all kinds of words that will fill the empty time and the beige space with meanings and colors. They'll want to come back because, in truth, they'll never really have to leave. Always sharing their verses and memories and stories. And to read those of others while they talk about what it means when they see or hear something they don't expect or that's so different from what they know, they have to think on it more. Isn't that what it would really be to have a congregation?"

He stared at her, unbelieving.

"This is the Way, Father. You know it is. You feel it too, deep in your bones."

He looked her up and down. "I, well, I don't think they would allow it."

She tilted her head. "They? The Goblins?"

"No, no, I mean, well, we have some important families in this town. You know, the goodly attendants who are always in the first pews, right up at the front of the church."

Cameo thought for a moment and then repeated five names she had been given as a warning. "Justus, Deacon, Charity, Clem, and Grace."

"Friends of yours?"

"Certainly not. But I also refuse to call them my enemies despite the past. That solution is simple, though. They all must now sit in the back. You will tell them that."

He laughed. "What? Why would I make such a rude demand?"

"It's not rude." She retorted. "It's necessary. They always sit in the front so that they can be seen. Now, they must be the ones asked to see. From the back, they will see differently. Maybe, they'll even notice."

"Notice? Let me guess. Notice you."

"That depends. Father, may I?"

"Dare I ask what?"

"Put a hold on those communion wafers. You'll get better absolution toasting marshmallows over tonight's campfire, anyway."

THE LONG WAY AROUND

Whew. At long last, I found the right voice. It only took another twenty years though.

When I was little, Ralph believed in God and went to church. When I was a teenager, Cameo didn't believe in God and didn't go to church. Now that the grass seems to be getting further away from me every year, I know that God believes in me again, and we sometimes meet up at the old saltbox parish in Patchling, Minnesota, when I visit my parents for Christmas. But you'd hardly even recognize either of us now.

The church is filled with voices every day, all day. Voices and words that spill out of its doors and travel down the sidewalk until they reach the corner diner or the old gas station on the edge of town. Some of them are singing, some of them are reciting verses and lines, or acting out plays in the garden next to Old Patch, the statue of the town's founder. Inside the narthex, there's a library where the barren classroom used to be, and it is an amazing sight to behold. Some of the books date all the way back to the founding of the church's original tradition in the Middle Ages, while others were written yesterday.

The pages of some will rip tears from your eyes, and others will make you laugh. Some talk of war, but more of them talk of the numerous homelands long since left behind in great-grandparents' generations. Most importantly, though, there are those that will boil your blood with fury. You will hate them. You will adore them. You will never stop thinking about them. I could spend hours there, touching my fingers to the beautiful Arabic calligraphy and trying to play from the sheet music of Norwegian folk-songs. I could sound out the Latin prayers and gaze in ecstasy at the Somali paintings. On one shelf, I may have even once spied the golden gilt spines of the Quran and the Torah, with bookmarks peeking out from their centers.

But what isn't there is fear. It's gone now because I took it with me when I left.

I gave it to the Goblins, while they were toasting marshmallows with old Father Olson and I in the woods.

"To what do we owe the visit?" They asked.

I told them, of course, and now they'll be paying back that debt for as long as I live. But not before the old preacher had gotten them to take all that he was 'bound' for, while splitting the difference of 'weather' between himself and the fieldstones. I know that sounds confusing, but it starts to make sense the more you think about how people talk.

Like how the Goblins also tried to get him to accept "soulless" but he took "solace" from them instead. How utterly Minnesotan of him to find the strength to withstand the next decade of sobriety by casually commenting on the forecast and his plans for the next potluck church dinner.

Unfortunately, the rest of my life had to take the long way around in the end. The struggle to free myself may have helped me to see the invisible chains that held my little town in bondage, but the scars left on my feet from the manacles I couldn't unlock meant that I had to return. I returned, and I returned, until I finally had everything I needed, and there was nothing left to come back to. When I had buried the last of my obligations and sold what was left, I knew that leaving was finally going to be permanent. That's when I went out to see them one more time.

"Say stray for more than a day and not one-y word." Forleer scowled at me. "We come to troll your lally, but no flies! Sharda we not palare more then."

Nine years since last I had been back, that was true. But I didn't know they'd been around my old house, seeing what bits and pieces they might arrange to summon me again.

"Magpies, all of you." I laughed. "But by the rules of the Crow's Market, I'm here for one last swap."

Ausgest stood up. "Left us with a debt no Goblins owes, you did. Parkered that nagging fear and walked on. Grows too fast to trade up or down."

"Yes, I know. But today, our battle ends." I said. "You have my surrender. My Cameo is yours to keep. Even up."

That was all it took. Versagen nodded. The three Goblins then gathered up their prizes and vanished into the undergrowth to celebrate with the ticks and mosquitoes. They had more than enough now to return victorious and have their names remembered.

There were no more Goblins seen in Patchling after that. The everywhere-brown finally sunk down beneath new green seedlings, and anything that couldn't grow on its own was planted with a row of petunias by the ladies' auxiliary. The corn came up on time. The cemetery finally got mowed. The clerk opened a painting studio. The church got a children's mural on the side facing the road. And written on the door in a flowy chalk hand was a set of nonsense verses. The verses were anonymous, of course, and no known author ever came forward, but then again, no one ever asked. The only question they did ask was what it meant. The new preacher, Justus Seaver and his wife Grace, two of the former back-row kids who'd just graduated from seminary the year before, would always just smile, though, and offer them the same question back.

Welcome ye gimpty tavs and those with
rooish frowl.
Set your mog upon the beck, put down
your airy sprowl.

Here we shum and jote and drod, till dibel
clangs to stop.
Then simbly comes and off we go, to
pumb, and luff, and fop.

Wholatry states but togranity hates, and
we will not estrange,
For sugracede is the better lede, with time
enough for change.

So, join us now with ferzy vim, and bring
your joyous glome,
None can take what knowside makes, or
cot your merry home.

GRANDMOTHER, I AM EARLY

I hope you never get old, she said.
Creaking knees raise a cloudy head.

And in my heart, I could not impart,
Kind stranger in a check-out line.
An insight unerringly divine.

I hope you never get old, she said.
Back bent to stop a shaking tread.

And in my mind, just too unkind,
Half her age of Fates' thread spun.
Damocles' sword a siphon.

It would be a privilege.
To see days of earned infirmity,
Not inflicted.
Stolen through hours of perfidy,
Uncontradicted.

I hope you never get old, she said.
Her words an aged curse dispatched.
She envied my smooth and redder cheek,
My tongue and words still attached.

But my misfortune stayed unseen.
As we each went about our day's routine.

Often, I'm told to not get old.
Just don't.

Don't worry, I say.
I won't.

THE VOICE AND THE VANGUARD

Religion is my poison. She sketched the delicately wet letters from the tip of a broken pen.

From morality's clotted spigot, I drink my virtue in.
From the ink-stained tongue of doctrine, I commit each and every sin.

Her coffee was already cold.

A childhood laced in cyanide, impurities distilled.
Drinking temptation's vintage, discontent refilled.

Just a sip to remind the waitress.

I found my true salvation, but not from begging to be blessed.
They sent me away from supper as I was not rightly dressed.

Excommunicate my body, and give fame to my disgrace,
Because now I spit my master's crumbs back into his face.

"Warm up, hun?"

"If you would please. Thank you."

There, I learned to build a chair.
My teachers proffered up the wood.

Forbidden books then built my tools.
Science joined, but tradition stood.

Too much sugar again. A little grit from the reused filter.

    I return, holding a scholar's decree,
    Paper for vestment's demands.
    But this table has no seat for me,
    So, I carry one now in my hands.

Hands tore through the page, ink bleeding through this table and blotting out printed two-ply napkins from advertising Piven's Diner. More of a commentary on the dessert selection than the drinks, really. It was just as well that she was thirty cents short for anything else on the menu, though. The coffee had delayed her long enough. The atonal rise and fall of the sirens keening past reminded her that forty-five minutes for two miles in the rain was already questionable this late at night.

So, she threw the pen into her bag. Hopefully, it would be a more useful memory than the coffee, and if she was lucky, it might even turn up again later right when she needed it. Sliding from the seat, she crumpled the stained napkins into the empty mug. Without the spoon to hold it back, her momentary musings unceremoniously ended the evening drowned by the dregs of an American medium roast.

As the woman left, the waitress maintained her air of concern from behind the relative safety of the lunch counter. More than once, her notepad acted as a retreat back to invisibility rather than poised in anticipation of a new order. The young woman had been kind enough, if aloof. She looked acceptably well but didn't act the part, somehow painfully out of place and inconspicuous all at the same time. The waitress thought her somehow unfortunate and, for a moment, offered the now empty seat a moment of compassion that perhaps its former occupant had been needing. She still scowled at the change left on the table though, wishing it were more.

Life had always expected more of Zachary than, it turned out, he was willing to give. Though it was not necessarily an uncommon situation for men of his age, he joylessly drifted from job to job, carefully avoiding the responsibilities that would land him solidly in the inescapable grip of adulthood. As a native Chicagoan, he had only ever read about Boston before moving to the South side, not far from Fort Point Channel, a few years ago. Even then, his expectations had been built up mainly through alternative weeklies and other kinds of artfully indifferent news as a place distinctly unexotic. But only because no one had ever figured out a good way to sell dockside fishnets romantically.

He preferred the transient atmosphere of the service industry anyway and, while he was always happy to take on long hours, he also liked the fact that he rarely saw the same face twice. His walk to work was always appealingly predictable. The maritime channel separating South Boston from the downtown area was popular with local artists and boasted a reasonably fashionable nightlife made up of floating art installations, live music bars, and seasonally popular history tours.

Despite the remaining evidence that the entire area had once been an active railyard, a decade of development had managed to turn the centuries-old colonial neighborhoods into a destination spot for travel pamphlets and tourist money. The remaining Revolutionary-era buildings still in view of the downtown skyscrapers, however, valiantly maintained their old orders. Even if they had mostly faded into weedy gardens slowly overtaking wilting houses. Behind the veneer of historical preservation, clapboard storefronts and storm-eaten churches dolefully mocked the restless harbor front down to their last chips of paint.

For Zach, it was the perfect hermitage for an occasionally recovered alcoholic like himself.

The Fort Pointe Shipyard catered to a younger crowd. Every Friday night, the usually placid bar and grill had been introducing themed music events loosely organized around its predominantly three-masted heavy frigate décor. As such, the Shipyard boasted craft beers, top-shelf imported mixers, and a signature crab dip with dill aptly titled Tidewrack.

In a dubious nod to the USS Constitution, a wood-hulled Navy vessel and museum anchored a few blocks down, the tables were scrap-stenciled from old radiator screens. The bar had also been recently renovated with wide, white oak floorboards and eland acanthus accents set against a herringbone background in gray, mauve, and brown. The Delft blue toile seat covers were, on the other hand, a hold-over from the most recent restaurant to fail in the same location.

But since they sported a somewhat vague pictoriagraphy resembling children playing with a toy boat, the owner hadn't seen much point in spending the money to reupholster them. With the low lights, it didn't really matter either way, and tonight's Mardi Gras party had necessitated covering most of the available surfaces with purple, green, and yellow foils to go with the band's gold harlequin bauta masks and fleur-de-lis top hats.

It was two hours and an unlit cigarette into his second shift. Already the customers were getting cocky, with wits sharpened on half-price shots, and the management predictably temperamental. Four boxes of extra Jack Daniels sat unopened in the back room, and the drunk on the third stool in was no longer drowned out by the incessant techno beats of DJ Soca Slam.

There was good money in it, but he hated Mardi Gras. It was the worst weekend of continuous festivities he could recall in his adult life, especially this far from New Orleans. Thankfully, the smile permanently decorating his face during happy hour was more than adequate to net him enough tips in three nights to pay rent, buy groceries, gas up, and settle in with enough knock-off science fiction movies to justify a fourth night in. He had also become immune to the consequences of plastic beads years ago, but the inevitability of spending at least four of his sixteen working hours cleaning up vomit was becoming the most tiring part of the ordeal.

"Another round over here, yeah?"

Halfway through a tray of two Black Russians, six margaritas, and a Jack and Coke was the first time he saw her. She was tall, dyed-black hair over her shoulders, and every strand completely out of place. She was uninterested in the revelry surrounding her, making her way through throngs of dancing college girls and cheering, stumbling, fraternity boys as quickly as the bouncing mass would allow. It was her strange state of dress that truly caught his attention. He noticed immediately that her white, button-down shirt was torn across the right sleeve, and it looked like her jeans had taken the brunt of a nasty collision with the pavement. A heavy coat hung over her right shoulder, and a scarred, leather mailbag clung to her side. For a moment, he thought she might have looked at him, but she then vanished into strobing beams of green and purple light.

A few minutes later, he caught a glimpse of her again, this time making her way slowly up the stairs to the balcony level. Glancing over her shoulder, he was certain that this time she stared directly at him. Her mouth was set in a firm line, much like the matching crease in her brow. Brown eyes glittered amber in the spray of lights. She turned again to sprint up the stairs past two girls in blue-spotted bikini tops.

He didn't see her again until he opened the back service door, hauling heavy, clanking bags of broken glass out to the dumpster in the alley. He swung the first over the edge and heard it clatter onto the rusty iron plates below. As he was about to swing the second bag, he felt his foot slip on something. Jumping back, one foot hopping with a foreboding sense of what might make such a sodden crunch, Zach spied the remains of a bird partially stuck to the bottom of his shoe.

"God dammit!" He swore, scraping his sole against the remaining bags. The plastic tore, leaving a sad, muddy smear of feathers stuck to the point of a green beer bottle. He sighed dramatically and rolled his eyes in resignation. Instead of continuing, he simply shook his head and lit up the cigarette he'd been holding in his shirt sleeve for the last few hours. Nothing was going right today anyway, so he figured nothing else ought to go right after this either. Exhaling slowly into the night, he glanced down at what little was left of the former bird.

A swirl of black tar and oil sported two stiff feet, curled around nothing but a bit of square foil confetti. The same Mardi Gras confetti that currently served as its plumage as well, though crumpled into shapes only vaguely reminiscent of the blue and chestnut feathers it had once had. The white of a paper-thin skull poked out just beneath a crest sticky with asphalt. The rest was just a congealed mess of trash blown in on the stench of low tide. He shrugged but for no one in particular. Waste among the waste.

"Hey!"

The sound jolted him out of himself, causing his heart to skip twice before finding a new rhythm. He dropped the cigarette and looked around, concern darkening his features. It was her. She was there, in the alleyway.

"You're the barman, right?"

He stared at her, scowling. Not intentionally, but mostly out of shock and confusion. She was small and stout, with the same disarray of white shirt and jeans as before. She had donned the coat, however. A thick, felt peacoat cut too long at the knees with the battered mailbag slung across her back. In the poor backdoor lighting, he also realized that her hair hadn't been dyed black but was, instead, dyed red at the ends. As if she'd tried to bleach it in a bathroom sink with little success.

"Uh, yeah," Zach replied, coming across somewhat dumbly. "You ok? Something wrong?"

"Yeah. Something's wrong." She stated flatly, hooks of sarcasm pulling at her mouth. "Can you get me to Mass General?"

"The hospital?"

"No, numb nuts, the nearest Catholic protest. Of course, the hospital."

"Look, lady, if something's wrong, you're injured or whatever, we can call 911 but..."

"Oh, for fuck's sake, I don't need an ambulance. I asked you if you could get me to Mass General. Like, now."

"Ok, you know what, I just work here, and I can't leave in the middle of a shift, ok?"

"What if it was life or death?"

"I'm sorry, what?"

"What if it was life or death? Would you do it then?"

"Is it, uh, is it life or death?"

"Yeah, it is."

He honestly didn't know how to feel. She obviously wasn't drunk or high and seemed completely in control of her faculties, but what she was saying felt so bizarre as to make Zach question whether or not he was hallucinating. Yet, he couldn't just turn away from her.

The intense stare in her soot-rimmed eyes held him in place just as sure as he'd been caught in a beacon from a lighthouse. Or headlights.

"There isn't time for this. Yes or no." She snapped.

"Wha...why do you need to go to the hospital?"

"Not your business. Take me there or don't. What'll it be?"

"Right now?"

"Right now."

Again, he was about to refuse, to make some excuse as to why returning to the chaos beyond the threshold was his only choice in the matter. For some reason, he found himself gesturing vaguely at the bird bones still sloughing off his shoe. When, suddenly, she spoke again.

"Zach!"

It was her voice. It was not her voice. It was the voice of something inhuman clinging to the stars above them. It tore through him until he felt his blood run red-hot and his breath evaporate into steam in his lungs. For a moment, he was breathing water again and being born. In a single syllable, he was unmade and remade, with a new name bestowed onto the resulting form that seemed strangely like the old one.

Except that it didn't mean the same thing. But because this new person had not yet learned anything of the world, he could only agree to what he was being asked to do. He reached into his pocket for his car keys and pointed to the old black car wedged into a no parking zone.

Finally, she smiled and made for the passenger side door. He blinked. In so doing, he noticed the trash bags but suddenly couldn't remember why he had brought them out into the alley. In fact, a wave of disgust greeted him at their sight. The smell was horrible, and it didn't seem like there was really anywhere for the bottles and napkins to go. So, he left them there, walking away with an odd sense that someone else would take it up where he had left off.

Before he reached the driver's side, however, he paused to turn back. It may have been the darkness or the uneven lines of the brick walls between buildings, but Zach was sure he could see a rather stately-looking bird happily preening on the edge of the dumpster lid. A sheen of oil-blue feathers crested over a chestnut breast and a white belly.

A kingfisher, ready to head off down the harbor in search of an early morning catch. When it looked up at him and fluttered, he almost dropped the key ring in his fingers, as a few flecks of purple and green foil twirled to the ground. Yes, he noted, the ground. Where springs of ivy were slowly making their way up the side of too many trash cans, and the black blooms of cold spring hellebores had taken the place of mangled Hefty draw-strings.

With an awestruck expression, he leaned in through the window at the strange woman now waiting patiently, hands folded, in the far seat of his car.

"Who are you?"

She looked at him with utter disinterest. "Éabha."

☙

They arrived at the hospital a few minutes after 11 pm, and no sooner had Zach skidded to a stop than Éabha was out of the car, moving with a determined stride to the main lobby doors. She had nearly made it all the way to the first-floor elevators by the time he caught up with her. As he reached out to catch her elbow, she pulled away with a look that was almost surprised to see him still there, but she didn't slow until they arrived at the main elevator. Éabha threw him a glance expressing her chagrin and tapped the up arrow impatiently.

"You should go." She stared intently at the lit floor indicators dinging slowly across the top of the doors.

"What the hell just happened back there!?" He pointed wildly in the general direction of the entrance doors.

She glanced at him again before returning to the row of lights descending downward.

"Listen, I don't have a lot of time, ok? Thanks for the ride. Really. But you need to go. Back to work or whatever."

"I'm not going anywhere until you tell me…" he was cut off as the elevator doors rumbled open, and Éabha jumped inside. Still running on adrenaline and nervous anger, he followed after her.

"Until you tell me what in God's name is going on here."

Éabha pressed the button for the 5th floor and sighed anxiously as the doors closed, drumming her fingers against the seam of her coat.

"I told you, Zach. I don't have time to explain it to you. You got me here in time. Thank you. I mean that, but that's all I can give you. It's important that I'm here right now, but if you don't get out of here, you're going to get yourself into trouble."

"What!? Why? What's going on? What kind of trouble are you in? Racing to your dying grandma's bedside before you get hauled off to prison or something?"

The elevator jerked to stop as the doors opened on a sterile, white hallway filled with nurses and monitors.

"Something like that." Éabha moved with a purpose, barely allowing the elevator to settle before breaking into a jog, dodging around an irritated nurse before taking the corner at a run.

Zach did his best to keep up, wary of the suspicious looks they were already gathering from the caretakers they passed. He did what little he could think of to make them seem less obvious, but he ended up offering only a few nervous smiles and a shrug to a passing therapist. He found Éabha at the end of the hallway, listening intently at the large, sliding glass door to room 512A. As he glanced around, it became apparent that they were in an intensive care unit of some kind. One where dedicated caregivers of all kinds were moving from station to station trying, with everything they had, to keep just one step ahead of Death itself. A ring of doors, the same as the one they stood before, circled a central nurse's station several feet away, punctuated by small nooks containing mobile computers and stacks of paper notations and graphs.

"What are you doing?" He hissed.

"Shhhh." Her brow pinched tightly over her forehead as she stood in deep concentration. "Yes, here." She said suddenly, shouldering past him as she pushed the door open and brushed through the privacy curtain. With a choked sound, he stumbled after her and immediately froze in horror.

Most of the room was entirely taken up by the bulky medical bed as well as numerous clicking machines and whirring motors. A mass of plastic tubes fed into a small, blanketed lump shrinking into the center of the mattress, a rhythmic wheeze of artificial air the only indication that what lay before him was even alive. The smell of formaldehyde and iodine permeated every corner of the cramped space and soaked into him with each breath he took. The lights in the room were off, splashing each angle and corner with patches of daisy-blue reflected from the streetlights outside the single, narrow window. He shuddered as he felt the walls close in around him, drowning him in a wave of despair routinely sanitized for clinical use.

Éabha came to stop at the foot of the bed and turned to face two small chairs tucked into the back wall. Zach also turned but instead saw two women staring back at them in shock, their eyes wide in worried confusion. The first woman was elderly, her white hair tied into a loose bun on the top of her head, her deeply lined face ragged and barren with many nights of mourning. She clasped her shaking hands around the shoulders of the second woman, who very much looked to be simply a younger version of her. The second woman, whose face also bore the swollen burdens of heartbreak, sat wrapped in a yellow baby blanket. Her T-shirt was creased with a few days of wear, and her long, brown hair hung limply around her.

Zach struggled with a dozen thoughts at once, trying to find the best way to explain their intrusion, but Éabha calmly rested her hand on the bar of the hospital bed and nodded.

"Christina?"

The women stared back at her for several breathless seconds before the younger woman finally broke, her voice raw and cracked as she spoke.

"My daughter?" She motioned toward the still form covered in white cotton.

Zach watched as Éabha stepped around to the bedside, pulling back the shroud to reveal the little girl quietly fading away in a stained nightgown. She couldn't have been more than ten years old, and her tiny body, ravaged by disease, lay shrunken and lifeless. Her hollow cheeks and bare head told him that the cancer had not yet ceased its steady, inevitable march through her, and the blackened circles around her eyes were all he needed to finally look away.

"Are you from hospice services?" The mother asked.

For the first time, Zach saw Éabha frown, a gentle expression that was at once both compassionate and strangely relieved.

"No." She replied. "But I don't want you to worry. Everything is going to be ok." The mother pursed her lips, puzzled.

"Zach." He started at the sound of his name. "If you're going to stand there, shut the door and pull the curtain all the way to the edge of the track."

"Uh, what?"

"Just do it."

The urgent command sent him into action for no other reason than he needed something to do, a function to calm his frayed nerves and convince himself that this invasion into the sanctity of the dying was somehow acceptable.

Éabha smoothed the ratty coat under her as she tenderly sat at the head of the bed. She reached underneath Christina, through the tubes and IVs, to slide her towards the edge before lifting her and cradling the fragile girl in her lap with one hand firmly beneath her head and the other resting over her chest.

"What are you doing?" The mother's worried tone prompted them both to look up from the stricken child.

Éabha appeared unwavering. "It's ok." She repeated, meeting the mother's uneasy scrutiny. "She's going to be ok."

The woman sputtered in oncoming outrage, sadness, and helplessness, lashing out at such an unwelcomed trespass into her pain. She readied a barrage at the cruel platitude when it suddenly and pitifully vanished from her throat, as though the indignation had been abruptly ripped out of her and thrown to the floor at her feet.

Zach felt the folds of the curtain slip through his hands as he turned to look at the mother, stock-still, her jaw slack and eyes growing steadily wider. Thick, unbelieving tears glinted in the low light as they seeped into the keepsake blanket still anchoring her to reality. He followed her eyes back to where Éabha sat, tilted forward over the girl in her arms, one hand still holding Christina balanced in her lap, the other now pressing into the girl's chest.

All at once, the medical indicators flickered, and the machines chirped subtle warnings, the readings on the screens beginning to fluctuate randomly. A sound filled the room, emanating, it seemed, from where Éabha and the girl sat. It started as a low hum, a haunting wind-like murmur pressing outward against the stillness. Zach thought he could hear voices in the wind, like hundreds of eager whispers crowding into the room, reaching out to be heard. He could feel the force of the sound, shaking the trays and chairs, causing the tubes and curtain to sway with the rhythm of the vibrations through the floor. Éabha looked only at the small girl, her face serene, unaffected by the disturbance building around her.

Zach steadied himself as best he could manage on one of the nearby chairs, tempted to call out to Éabha and wake her from her meditation. But no matter how hard he tried, he couldn't make a single noise. Every attempt he made seemed to dissipate before he could get it out. The temperature in the room was becoming uncomfortably hot, and he could see shimmers of energy ripple through the scalding air.

The sound amplified until it became a pulsating tempo of distant voices raised in a peculiar, layered harmony. It continued to grow stronger, building in cadence and meter until Zach was certain that the room would flash over and burn by the sheer weight of each surge. He felt panic rising in his chest as each breath seared his lungs, and the crushing sound made the room bend and lurch.

He lost his footing reaching for the curtain and tried frantically to scramble for the door, no longer able to even make out the two women or Éabha only a few feet away. He rolled onto his back to shield his face from the onslaught when a piercing light split the air.

White, blazing consciousness, awakened everywhere, within everything.

It rendered him momentarily insensible, sucking the heat and song from the room with a blinding flare. The unworldly radiance ravaged the room. Bright rays raced across the ceiling until it had filled every dark corner and empty space with brilliant colors. There was a sound like a great cry, the sound an infant makes when it is born and a mother makes when it is no more. A song of tone and vibration, a fusion of souls in sonorous reverberation. Zach could be nothing else but shaken to his core.

Forever and a moment later, the light began to recede, to fade back into inoffensive pastel hues. Zach dared a look at Éabha and the girl still seated on the deathbed. He watched in terrified astonishment as the light bathed the little girl, saturating her tiny arms and legs and pouring into her thin body. He trembled as the sound finally coalesced into a single, pure note that, he could now see, came from Éabha herself.

She held the girl tightly to her shoulder, rocking slowly back and forth, her head thrown back as she sang out in a voice that did not seem to be possible. The note shattered into a dozen wrenching melodies as she sang to the girl, weeping through each beautiful lilt of an unearthly lullaby whose words he could not understand.

Struggling to his feet, Zach tried to take it all in. The light, which had so swiftly cut through the grief, winked out. The song that Éabha sang waned into a soft hum before ending in a sudden breath, as she came back to herself with a shock. She paused to look down at the girl before looking up at Zach with an expression he couldn't quite define. She looked tired and sad but somehow content.

"Christina!"

The mother shoved past Zach as Éabha held the girl out for her.

"Christina!" she grabbed hold of the girl and tore the blankets from her face.

In that instant, the room ceased to breathe, ceased to beat, falling into an overwhelming hush. Christina, who only moments ago had prepared to breathe her last, blinked awake from her sleep, held securely in her mother's arms. Her plump cheeks rounded into a drowsy smile as her mother's shaking hands sifted disbelievingly through short, ginger locks. Her sallow, sickly skin had given way to a rosy flush, and the limbs that stretched sleepily out from the blanket were soft and full.

For as long as he would live, Zach would never forget the sound of that mother's cry.

As Christina stifled a second yawn, the two women looked to Éabha, their hands furiously wiping at their faces to see her through the tears. Éabha rose to her feet with a smile, meeting the mother's babbling lips with a raised hand.

"All I ask is that you say nothing." She said, her voice low. "Please. If you value this miracle, protect it. Say nothing of me or what you have seen and heard here tonight."

Through a gasping sob, the mother nodded, her eyes and mouth wracked with renewed tears, filling her words with too much salt to keep them long enough on her tongue. She clutched the little girl closer as she put her hand out to grasp Éabha's arm.

"Tell no one. Please. That's the price you must pay for what you've been given. Do not name it. Do not speak it."

"Won't" She coughed out. "I won't. Thank you, Oh God, Thank you, Thank you. My baby, thank you. I don't even.... I can't...I don't..."

With a nod to the three huddled around the bed, Éabha walked quickly back to the sliding door and peeked past the curtain to check the hallway. Satisfied that the events that had just transpired had somehow gone unnoticed, she slid out of the room without a backward glance. For the third time that night, Zach found himself dashing after her, muttering something incomprehensible to the gathered family before sprinting past.

⁓∂℮⁓

Zach never saw Éabha again after that night. The hallway was empty when he ran out. No one from the nurses' station to the reception desk had any memory of who he described, and the woman with the pale red ends never reappeared. But then again, he also never went back to The Fort Pointe Shipyard, and he never took another drink of alcohol ever again.

71

Not because he actively refused any of it, but rather it simply never occurred to him after that night. Instead, he found that his words actually meant something to those whose struggles were just like his. That when he spoke, they listened. And when they listened, they sometimes found healing, too.

For years, Zach would come to marvel at the very fact that all it took was just a simple series of sounds, made into words, to change everything for someone else. He never knew exactly which sounds or which words, but by putting them all out there, he could watch their light spread from one person to the next.

The fearful part of him worried that he'd once witnessed a true miracle and that he'd spend the rest of his life chasing after every lead that might bring him back to that miracle again. But he didn't. The miracle, as it turned out, had decided to stay with him for a while. On his worst days, the kingfisher would come to perch on his apartment balcony.

Checking in on him when the skies grew stormy and grey. But each time the bird appeared, Zach funnily found himself reassuring his little feathered friend in return. Morning would always be there waiting for them, he would say, just as soon as they woke up.

⁓∂θℓ⁓

The body must be painted, dyed. She wrote. And then it is made to bleed.

Another beer certainly wouldn't do anyone any harm, she thought, raising her hand and pointing to the empty glass.

Sometimes beauty, sometimes sin. Well, that line wasn't as good. Never will I concede. No.

The social skin is dyed.

By beauty made with stick and pin;

On second thought, it was already past ten, and the regulars were all that was left at this particular local bar.

This palimpsest my scars control, What is without must be within, but always more because the soul, Is not reflected by our skin.

With a grimace, Éabha scribbled the verse out and started over.

Agony revised sublime. A palimpsest of scars to date; it's irony I cannot write. All I can do is annotate!

Even worse.

The woman next to her, slowly nursing a white cream drink, leaned over and craned her neck to get a better look at the loopy cursive spanning two napkins and a coaster.

"Hey." She nodded, indicating the blotched scribbles. "That's pretty good. You a writer?"

"No. I have dermatographia."

"What? What's that?"

"Nothing. I just have a problem with words." She answered, but then paused, as if listening to a voice no one else could hear.

"What is it? Are...are you ok?" The other asked.

Looking over the petite Asian woman in her bland polo shirt, Éabha pushed her glass away and turned the barstool to face a curious but cautious expression. "What's your name?"

72

"Ah Cy." She chuckled with a sad tint to her laughter. "But everyone calls me Grace. I work in HR." She pointed to the logo stitched to the front of her ill-fitted uniform. "Less confusion, they tell me. Or because it sounds too much like...well, anyway. Just here for a team-building exercise, I guess. Or something to that effect. You?"

Éabha scowled, glancing backwards to note that a group of similarly dressed office workers were currently circling a table, though it didn't escape her that the one they chose left no empty seats for the hunched figure at her side. She turned back to Ah Cy.

"Can you get me to University Park Hospital?"

"Right now?"

"Right now."

LACRIMOSA

I could not leave my body,
I stayed behind to watch,
My hair began to wither,
And my skin began to blotch.

Standing for my funeral,
To comfort those who mourn,
I take their tears now with me,
But their platitudes I scorn.

When I died, I stayed inside,
Long after I was bones,
Until the grass grew out my mind,
And my eyes and ears were stones.

When all of this had come to pass,
At last I moved beyond,
I simply had to see the wake,
Where all I was had gone.

PUMPKIN-HEART THE HALLOWEEN CAT

Emma Mildred Montrose was such a great name. So were Julian Jefferson Montrose and Montrose Cricket Sunday. She rearranged the photo frames again so that each cat would be lined up on the piano according to the year they were born. Almost twenty in all, the first five were in black and white. The sixth, barely in color at all, was faded well into a Polaroid yellow.

The rest had been retouched in the years since she had first collected the pictures from old albums in the basement. Now, they were all there for her to keep and enjoy once more. Every cat she had ever been blessed to have, looking back at her warmly, irritably, and snidely from atop a set of keys her hands were too arthritic to play anymore.

June Philips-Montrose however, was not a particularly great name. She hated it actually. Her parents had thought it cute to name her and her two eldest sisters after months of the year. Hence April, May, and June Philips had each graced the late 1930s with birthdays that were not even remotely in spring or summer.

In fact, June had been born on Halloween night and was thoroughly convinced that she had been cheated out of a truly memorable would-be name. Something coy or mischievous, befitting her personality, like Lucy or Charlotte.

So, she had given all her favorite names to her cats instead. The only companions who had ever come to see her and comfort her in the loneliness of dotage. But now, they were all gone too; taken by old age and sickness. Except for the last one, Sayona. She had simply wandered out the door one day and had never come home.

The bell chimed loudly in the foyer and June couldn't help but smile and rush to the front door. It was Halloween again after all, and the neighborhood trick-or-treaters would just now be starting their rounds. She had two bowls prepared, sitting on the small table in the entryway.

One filled with full-sized candy bars and the other piled up with packets of crayons, sidewalk chalk, and wind-up whirligigs. She had even moved one of the dining room chairs onto the rug, so that she could sit and wait while the next group came bouncing up the front stoop to ring the bell. It was her birthday, and this was the best treat she could imagine.

With a grin, she threw open the door and yelled "Happy Halloween!" to the delighted screams of several superheroes and a homemade felt pumpkin.

Her eyesight wasn't all that good anymore, so she relied on the sounds of squeals and hops to ensure that each goblin and ghost assaulting her porch was thoroughly satisfied before wailing off back into the darkness.

She also made sure to wave to each voice that yelled "Thank you, Mrs. Montrose" from the yard. Some she recognized, most she didn't.

It hardly mattered though. The joy quickly spreading down the street was all she could have asked for and she was content to remain in her macabre bubble of annual bliss for one night a year. The loneliness could come back tomorrow. For three hours, she was dazzled by the lights and the costumes and for three hours she clapped happily along with high-pitched shouts of "Trick or Treat!"

She was also sure to ask each child what they had chosen to go as this year and to lean down as far as her creaky old knees would allow for the smallest and shyest ones to get their candy too. It was a birthday party, she reminded herself, and everyone should be allowed to attend. Cake, candles, presents, laughter; holding on to it because in just a few seconds, it would be blown out. And then, nothing but quiet as the next year crept in from under the eaves.

Too quickly though, the darkness returned as the stars arched above, then winked out. June sat in her chair and huffed, just a little out of breath from all the wonderful activity. She chanced a look up at the clock on the wall and could just make out the hands at ten and twelve. It was getting late, and the stream of little devils and demons was drying up. Her bowls were almost empty. She mustered a smile and wondered if maybe she ought to leave the rest out on the top stair of the porch. Someone might come by for the last candy bar or two, even if it was just an unexpected treat for the mailman in the morning.

The doorbell chimed one more time.

She gripped the bowl and immediately stood up. What perfect timing and such an auspicious way to end the night. But when she opened the door, there was only one child standing there, dressed in the tatters of a too-old fox costume he must have grown out of at least two years ago. He was a small boy, probably around eight or nine years old, holding a cheap plastic pail in both hands as he stared glumly at the decorations.

"Happy Halloween!" June exclaimed in her usual ebullient manner. The boy glanced up at her and then back down again.

"Trick or treat?" She offered, in a more genial tone.

He simply pointed at her round plant-stand near the door. The one she had cleared off for a brand-new cat skeleton decoration she had gotten at the local hardware store. It was cheaply molded and made from an off-white resin, with a jaw articulated by painted screws. She had also arranged her new Halloween cat atop a pile of tiny orange and white pumpkins from the farmstand, placing the tiniest one inside the ribcage to weigh it down against the wind. Otherwise, it was so light it would have just skittered away down the walk with every gust.

"Is that Pumpkin-Heart?" The boy asked.

June looked around a little worriedly but soon spotted who she assumed to be the boy's mother standing at the bottom of the porch next to the posts. She too was ill-dressed for the cold weather and pulled her threadbare sweater-wrap around her shoulders tighter.

"I, well..." June started but then gathered herself with a little imagination. "Why sure. That's Pumpkin-Heart all right. The Halloween cat!"

The boy nodded, still clutching his bucket. But then, as if a deluge had broken a dam, a flood of words poured out of him all at once with barely a breath in-between them.

"Yeah, it's Pumpkin-Heart. I know him, you know. He comes every year to stalk the neighborhoods and steal kids' candy after they get it. This is because, you know, one day Pumpkin-Heart got lost, and because he wasn't wearing a collar, he became a stray and died because no one would let him into their house anymore. So now he comes back every Halloween to steal the sweets from trick-or-treat houses so that he can give them to ghost children who will play with him and then he won't be a stray because he'll have kids who love him again."

June blinked in surprise, but the boy just barreled on.

"And if he can't find the ghost children, he visits all the lost and stray pets in the town and, if they are good boys and good girls, he might just take them back home again. And yeah so, for like a hundred years, Pumpkin-Heart the Halloween Cat has appeared one night a year to steal candy for the ghost children and to lead lost strays back to their families. All because he can't find his own way home."

"I...I'm so sorry." His mother suddenly interjected, coming up behind her son as he fell silent once more. "We, uh, we recently lost our cat, and this is his story about why he hasn't come home. He's gone to be with Pumpkin-Heart, you know, and all the other lost pets."

"Yeah!" The boy agreed loudly, once again motioning towards the plastic cat. "And Pumpkin-Heart hides all the candy in his pumpkin heart, like that one right there. Otherwise, it would just fall out of his ribs."

"Well then." June coughed and straightened. "How about you take both of these candy bars with you. Just in case Pumpkin-Heart steals one."

For the first time in those three short minutes, the boy looked up at her with a small smile and put the candy into his pail.

"Thanks." He said, and promptly walked away. His mother shrugged with a sheepish look and followed after him.

But June stood there on her porch, the icy wind prickling through her thin clothes, completely stunned. It had been nothing more than a flash of a moment, and now she couldn't stop thinking about the story the unknown boy had just told her. She looked over her shoulder at what had previously been an impulsive after-thought, a fun addition to her menagerie of cat-related accessories. Now, it suddenly seemed like something much more. Pumpkin-Heart the Halloween Cat, staring back at her with empty eye sockets and a Cheshire grin.

She sniffed as her nose began to run. "If that's true," she waved her empty bowl at the pile of otherwise useless gourds. "Then..." Her bottom lip trembled. "Maybe I can see Sayona again tonight, eh? Yes? No? "Oh, nevermind."

The plastic decoration naturally did not respond, and she sighed, walked back into the house, and turned off the lights; blowing out the candles on her eighty-sixth year at last.

All, it seemed though, except for one.

An eerie blue flicker moved from underneath the rose bushes, a jack-o-lantern from across the street momentarily illuminating the highlights on old, pocked, bones. Dried sinews crunched and withered joints creaked as the small feline skeleton stole quietly onto the bottom stair.

A pair of empty eye sockets, whose darkness reflected the missing stars back in tiny pinpoints of dim light, regarded his own effigy with a mixture of curiosity and mistrust. The strange plastic frame had molded plastic ears, after all, and a tail clearly twice too long. His own ears were barely wisps of candle-wick smoke and his tail was broken. But then a tootsie roll fell from his ribs and the apparition was obliged to pick it up and put it back into his ethereally beating pumpkin heart.

He tried to meow, but it was only a grim rasp akin to the rustling of leaves. He tried again, but the lights in the window did not return. Instead, Pumpkin-Heart observed as some nineteen ghostly cats all began to gather on the windowsills looking out. Some were plump and long-haired as they had been in life while others were faded into a dim grey, barely visible between their brighter siblings. He tilted his skull to regard them since their dried or misaligned eyes all tried to give him pleading looks.

"One is missing." He heard the ragged tabby say. Whispering with long syllables as the dead tend to do. "We can't go yet. One is missing."

"Yes." The mummified orange and white tom agreed. "Missing."

"Help us." The ashen tuxedo hissed. "She must find her way back. Too cruel to leave her behind."

"One is missing." A balled-up kitten, sparkling with frost, repeated from beneath the porch stairs.

Pumpkin-Heart appraised them all over, looking well and waiting. Then, he dipped his head once, flexed his fish-hook claws, and rattled back out into the yard. No one paid him any mind as he slinked along in the grass or down below the curb, because it often seemed as if no one could see him. He moved as a normal cat would but the thin skeleton and arched spine no more than the width of a bottleneck ought to have given him away if anyone had taken the honest time to notice.

He passed Paisley sitting on her memorial stone in the Johnson's front garden, and Luna, dead now for more than a year, conversing with Oreo, the Harris' new housecat who'd slipped out the front door again. Then, Millie and Max, still eternally running around an abandoned playhouse that must have been sitting in the back woods for more than a decade while Ginger snoozed, forever, on the rocking chair creaking in the corner of Old Man Simon's patio.

They all gave a slow blink as he passed by, just as they did every year, but that was all. None had any reason to call on Pumpkin-Heart on this night or any other. He headed south, down the road until it became small rocks and gravel, toward the lakeshore where the waters were stained black all around the shoreline. He came here often, in fact. Mostly to sit with Jimmy and to watch him throw skipping stones that never skipped. Jimmy was about twelve years old, sitting on the edge of a dock that had long ago sunk into the mud beneath the shallows.

Only its main support pillars now remained just above the water's surface and the elder townsfolk still sometimes stopped by it along the road to reminisce about their own childhoods. Jimmy had drowned beneath that dock back in 1958 and because no one had known where he was at the time, his bones remained mixed with the driftwood more than a foot under the muck.

Now, he just skipped stones and waited. His sister was seven years older than him, and he figured she ought to be along soon. And he also had Pumpkin-Heart, patting the old creature on the head as the cat came to sit next to him in the usual way, bony pelvis balanced on his pile of rocks. The tootsie roll dropped out again, but this time Jimmy picked it up, unwrapped the candy with glee, and tossed it into his mouth.

"I went as a cowboy last year, you know." He said, chewing sloppily through the melting chocolate. "Dad promised we'd get ponies for Christmas, so we all 'ad to look right 'fore then. Laura was the only one'd got a pony though. Guess they cos' too much. S'ok, I liked the Lincoln Logs. Wonder what happen'd to 'em?"

Pumpkin-Heart pawed at the boy's overalls.

"N'ah. I'm not wantin' to play right now. Sorry, Punk'n."

The Halloween Cat caught a claw in the denim and rasped loudly, turning his rictus face back towards the highway.

"Oh, I see. Ya lookin' for somebody. Ya gotta ask Beth Ann then. She's the only one who watches the road right now."

Pumpkin-Heart nodded and pulled two butterscotch candies out from his ribs, much to Jimmy's delight. He'd have to save the Arcor Strawberry bon bons for Beth Ann, though. She'd lost the memories of everything else.

Thus, with cautious steps, careful not to disturb any sentinel cicada husks, Pumpkin-Heart left the side of the lake and returned to the road. Cars still occasionally raced by; their high headlights too bright to spot him in the grass and his bones too motionless to be noticed by inattentive drivers. But he knew where he was going despite the blasts of careless wind and exhaust.

Soft clicks of bone paws tapped across the asphalt for over a mile, his short vertebral tail swishing thoughtfully through the dried blades of brown ditch grass. A thin layer of ice had even begun to form on the marshy waters of the cistern. Barely two inches deep, the frogs within had either fled or were already dying in the cold. But on the rise, a rickety cross stood in silent vigil over a sharp curve in the road.

Here, in 1971, seventeen-year-old Beth Ann Farley had been struck and killed by a drunk driver as she walked home from her friend's farm. A makeshift plaque nailed to the wooden cross explained as much, though the pink and blue fabric flower-wreath that had once adorned the memorial was now lying face down in a bush and had rotted down to few twigs tied together with wind-knotted thread. Discarded beer cans and cigarette butts were now all that decorated her shrine.

Beth Ann herself sat quietly near the cornstalks, ghostly wisps of her hair breaking away like the silk on unharvested cobs. She smiled as her mother's voice called her name from across the field, telling her over and over that it was time for supper. She would go soon, to meet up with her parents and her big lumpy labrador, Sophie. To smell the bread baking and to hear the cows complaining. But there was one more person she had to see before then and he hadn't been back yet. The man from the car, with his eyes wide and his mouth open in a shocked scream. He would though, eventually. It was unavoidable since all the paths of his life had already led back to here in one way or another.

Pumpkin-Heart bounded over the strewn trash to rub his head affectionately against her legs. His purr coming from the vibrating sinews of his neck still dried and stuck to a partial collarbone that fluttered against his sternum.

Beth Ann reached out and scratched her fingers along his spine. "Hey there, Pum." She whispered through the holes in her cheek with air drawn in through the wound in her chest. "What brings you all the way down here? Houses are too far apart on this side for trick-or-treaters. Nobody wants to walk two miles up every driveway."

The bony old cat scratched at the ground and clattered his teeth. Circling, ever circling, around and around her feet. He then cast his bluish gaze out onto the road again, looking back at her for an answer.

"Someone's gotten themselves lost then, eh? Well, I haven't seen anything. I did hear something awhile back though. Too long ago now for hope, I think. Down by the first bend. You know how people take that turn. Never even think twice about what might be on the other side of those trees."

With a gentle grasp of his brittle teeth, Pumpkin-Heart pulled a strawberry candy from his ribcage and pressed it onto her hand. For a moment, Beth Ann became a little brighter, her face less bleak and broken.

"I remember these things!" She laughed. "My grandma had a candy dish that was always full of 'em! Little foil strawberries probably older than I was. I thought I was so clever back then though, stealing them out of the dish when no one was looking. Nana knew, of course. Because she always quietly came back and put more in. Reminds me of summers at her house."

As the girl crinkled the wrapper in her palm and touched the candy to her shattered nose, Pumpkin-Heart grated out his goodbye and trotted off further along the side of the road. There he encountered a few crickets and one very confused parakeet but continued on until he spied the back of another spectral cat, facing away from him, with her head bowed and her ears drooping.

Beneath the wraithy tabby, the patch of grasses grew taller than the ones around it, with tiny purple blooms on thin stalks that arched out like a spider's legs, from ribs crushed into the dirt. From the ruined skull, mushrooms slowly froze against the eye sockets. For months now past, they were the only reason that anything at all remained in this nowhere space by the roadside. Everything else had been carried off by the beetles and mice.

Soon though, she would disappear beneath the snow and then disappear completely into the muddy run-off of the lakeshore bank. Such was the fate of all cats who died on the side of road. In the brush in front of her, however, something actually was moving.

Pumpkin-Heart strode over to where Sayona was sitting, matching her gaze to observe a small orange cat hunched near a rock. His back paw was terribly twisted and the deep scrapes across his haunch bore witness to the wheel of another unmarked car. His breathing was heavy and pained, his nose buried in the ruff of his chest so that he would not have to look back at the sightless skull staring back at him, portending his fate. All he could feel was the lancing agony through his side and all he could see was Death grinning at his misfortune.

He hadn't meant to get lost. He'd only wanted to follow those little lights dancing in the field. How was he to know that the far side of the land was cut off by a road and that the lights weren't dancing in the wildflowers at all, but rushing past faster than a sparrow could fly? He thought they might have been moths or fireflies or paper flutters on the end of a string.

He raised his head and cried. But it was no use. His throat was dry, and he was far too tired to manage more than a plaintive sob. His boy couldn't hear him.

The ghost of Sayona kept her vigil, even as Pumpkin-Heart came to sit beside her.

"This is a bad place." She said. "I've seen the pile of claws down under here. Soon, I will join them. He will follow me. And then the next one will come, and the lights will burn them out too."

"Is that why you wait?" Pumpkin-Heart asked. "You wait for him?"

"I was alone. I don't want him to be alone too."

"But it is the very fact that you are here that frightens him."

She pricked the shapes of her ears. "Does he not see me comforting him?"

"Only emptiness."

"My gentle reassurances?"

"Only silence."

"But I am here!"

"And he is not."

Sayona raised her head, her eyes watery and still. "Then I am alone too. Here we are in the very same place, deserted. Abandoned even by our own shadows."

Pumpkin-Heart strangely agreed. But then continued. "Don't mind this one. Come with me. I have brought lemon balm and roses from the old woman's garden to lay over your body. She picked them for you and left them on the porch, in a pile of her pumpkins of course."

"June lady." Sayona sighed. "We'd play in her plants and baskets every year when she put them out, but she'd never yell at us. She would cook birds and give each of us a piece. Her blankets were always warm, no matter what the sky did. I miss her. I miss the magic fire on the stones that she could conjure. She was so powerful that it didn't even dare try and leave its iron cage. I miss June lady."

From his ribs, Pumpkin-Heart pulled free the promised blooms and set them each down, stem by stem, onto the remains of the lost little girl-cat. No more a tabby now but skin and bones stained black with each passing wash of tar. The frightened orange cat seemed perplexed at the bundle that came rolling in on the wind and caught in the bones near his feet. It smelled light and fresh, with a minty tinge that drew him towards it. He tried to rise but stumbled, pain shooting through him with fierce intensity. But that smell, it just seemed to...make it all a little better.

"Sayona." The skeleton cat said. "It's time to go."

And so, two cats walked along the edge of the road at night. One a stiff articulation of bones grasping onto the rocks with tightly sinewed claws and the second, a bouncing whisper of mist as light as a feather on the breeze. Their eyes were the reflections of porch lights on the water and their passage through the tall grasses bent the blades only as far as the wind could.

But when they arrived back on the paved streets of their nondescript hometown, all was still and silent. The last few jack-o-lanterns flickered out the remnants of their wax candles on empty steps while linen ghosts and velvet spiders slipped back into windows and crawled beneath locking doors.

The house of June Philips-Montrose however, stood as a beacon of welcome. Garlands of black and orange wrapped around the rails and threaded through the lattice work. Piles of leaves artfully gathered around the front yard, with pumpkins holding court at their centers. And, of course, a plastic bone cat on the mail stand near the front door. Its back arched and tail raised as if in perpetual fright. A packet of candy tarts had been left by its feet where its little pumpkin heart had already fallen out and rolled off onto the door mat.

Sayona looked up at the windows with unexpected sadness. She thought she should be overjoyed to find her way home at last and all of the other cats had even gathered about the sills and plant stands to see her return. One even twitched the end of her tail, as if to say that it was about time.

"You're not happy." Pumpkin-Heart stated.

"No, I am." She replied, turning her head down to observe her paws dissolving in the auras of drug-store fairy lights. "But...I've only come to a house. To a place where I used to live. June lady won't know I'm here. June lady won't see me. Even if I jump up onto the bed. If I can't feel finger-thumbs on my nose, how can it be home?"

Pumpkin-Heart's neck creaked as he raised his face to consider the gathering, the strangely quiet and unusual peace in a house of cats. Without any other acknowledgment, he left Sayona on the porch, jumped up along the handrails, and then to the gutters, until he found his way into the house through a break in the attic gable.

From there, it was a rhythmic bit of tip-tapping across the hall in time with the ticking of the downstairs clock. Then, it was over the bedroom threshold and onto a field of daisies stitched across the top of a down duvet. Yellow threads caught in the rough, dried, pads of his ruined paws but for the first time that night, Pumpkin-Heart curled his bare tail back and forth with anticipation.

June was fast asleep, her face relaxed in the repose of a dreaming slumber. The scenes that danced across her eyes were awash in sunshine, on a day that had passed by her seven decades ago.

A little girl was playing in a stream, getting dirt on the Easter dress her mother would scold her for later. But it was spring, and the mud was in perfect supple form for making her tiny sculptures of horses and gnomes. In her own little paradise, far away from the rest of the world, she could create anything she wanted out of the weeds and slime.

Reed huts for miniature clay people to live in with roofs decorated by algae, duckweed, and cattail fluff. Barns for the horses made from pebbles and a silo made from a discarded soda can so old that it gleamed pure silver in the sun. Joyous, the little girl laughed and got cockleburs in her pigtails but the shadows that skirted the edges of the dream began to encroach, and the ditch weeds sharpened, as if to overtake her.

Pumpkin-Heart did not like what he saw in the darkness surrounding her. He saw threads, like spider silk, clinging onto her and vanishing into the spaces beyond. But they were not attached to trees or anything like a forest beyond the stream. They were attached to other memories, of other Junes, as they spun around and around her. There was June on her wedding day, looking somber and unsure; older women crushing in around her with good-wife admonitions she didn't understand.

There was June as a young mother, sitting at the kitchen table sobbing while an infant screamed in the distance. And then June the secretary, trying to hide her neck beneath a button-down sweater as her boss stopped at her desk for the tenth time that day. But it was June, alone at the window, that exerted the strongest pull. Two weeks next to her own mother's deathbed she had said none of the words she had meant to, and now they ate through her soul. It all began to spin faster, entangling the little girl as ribbons might a maypole.

Everything became a blur of expectations that only partially seemed as though they came from June herself. Pumpkin-Heart felt himself waver again, as though he stood on some unsteady precipice that would give way with the slightest uncertainty. But he wasn't frightened. The far depths weren't a terrible place to go. Just quiet. Just away. Just one more step through the archway to the ledge but then he saw them.

The cats. Nimbly, they pounced on loose threads, catching the ends in their teeth and holding tight. Or balanced carefully on thin wires, acrobatically moving from one line to the next. Others set to chewing the attachments, as bonds they could break with sharp teeth and determined claws. They were, of course, her cats. Protecting her now as they always had in the past.

He saw the zoetrope around him begin to roll and play out its recorded time. A life lived in the silhouettes someone had placed in the lunette cut-outs, but it was June who was the light at the center. And always around her, the shape of a cat; A tuxedo beneath the hem of her white gown to reassuringly rub against her ankles, a tabby in the crib to soothe her babies, an orange tiger-stripe who prowled the office of her old boss, who was allergic to cats, so that he could never quite figure out why he coughed and wheezed his miserable way through each day.

And then there was Midnight, the black cat who had come to see her mother off into forever-sleep, and to remind June that life burbled on, in a steady stream of purring while he warmed her lap. It was then Pumpkin-Heart noticed that Sayona had picked her way from the bottom stairs to that same threshold between sleep and morning. She had hopped down from the daisy duvet and onto a log that led to a little girl angrily pulling her shoes out of the muck.

When she mewed loudly, the girl looked up and smiled.

"Well, hello there, kitty! Are you lost?" She stretched out her fingers towards Sayona's ears and the cat happily leaned in for her favorite scratches, from a hand she missed so very much. "Nice kitty!"

Sayona purred happily and pressed her head as hard as she could into the small hand. The girl giggled, and without a moment's hesitation, sat straight down into a grassy puddle. Her tights and dress stained beyond repair; it was as if she were finally freed. Her white church clothes drunk up the sodden swamp, quenching their raging thirst with grime. But from there, she patted her knees until Sayona had jumped down from the log and come to rest on the hammock she'd made of her lacey skirt, where the cat could be petted and kissed in earnest.

"Oh, you're so sweet." She whispered. "I missed you so so much. I thought you were gone forever. I thought you were all gone forever!"

Through the marsh, the other cats began to trickle in. They set down their threads and stopped chasing every loose bit of memory, to turn back toward the sunshine and bask in the warmth of the summer light. Nearly twenty in all, and a small kitten thawing in the heat of her hand.

They played with the floating thistledown and tumbled over each other to get the next round of belly rubs. They kneaded her leg and forced their faces beneath her elbows. She laughed and buried her cheek against furry ruffs as everything else dutifully receded. Old Junes called out but were ignored. Finally, they began to fade.

The memories then departed but they left her love behind, giggling in a backwoods stream. This was because June Philips-Montrose had put it in her will, that when all that was left was her was love, they were to give it away. To let go of it. To give it to children and the elderly. To the lonely.

Whatever was left of her should be given to all those who needed it most and who had never once heard her name.

The last shadow to remain regarded them all without expression. The skeleton cat briefly lamented his lack of ears to tug or fur to tousle, but his pumpkin heart trembled in time with the sound of slowing breaths. It really did look like such fun down there, but he understood that June did not want to leave her favorite place. And Pumpkin-Heart was not about the make her. Instead, he let her stay and left with the few years she had remaining.

June had but five years more. Five years she happily gave to another soul, limping down a deserted road and crying loudly for his family to find him. An orange cat that, just a few moments ago, was certain that he'd met his end. Staring into the empty skull of his own imminent future, crushed beneath a speeding truck, now just feeding the ants and creepers.

But then, he'd been granted another life; maybe his second, maybe his third. That very skeleton cat had suddenly stood up, dragged him to his feet, and sent him off back towards the lights on the far side of the lake.

Or, at least, that was the story the boy told his mother the morning their missing cat, Pumpkin, finally reappeared at the back door. It was the day after Halloween, and he had a badly injured leg. The poor cat was also rough and coated with dust, but his fur oddly smelled of lemon and rose petals.

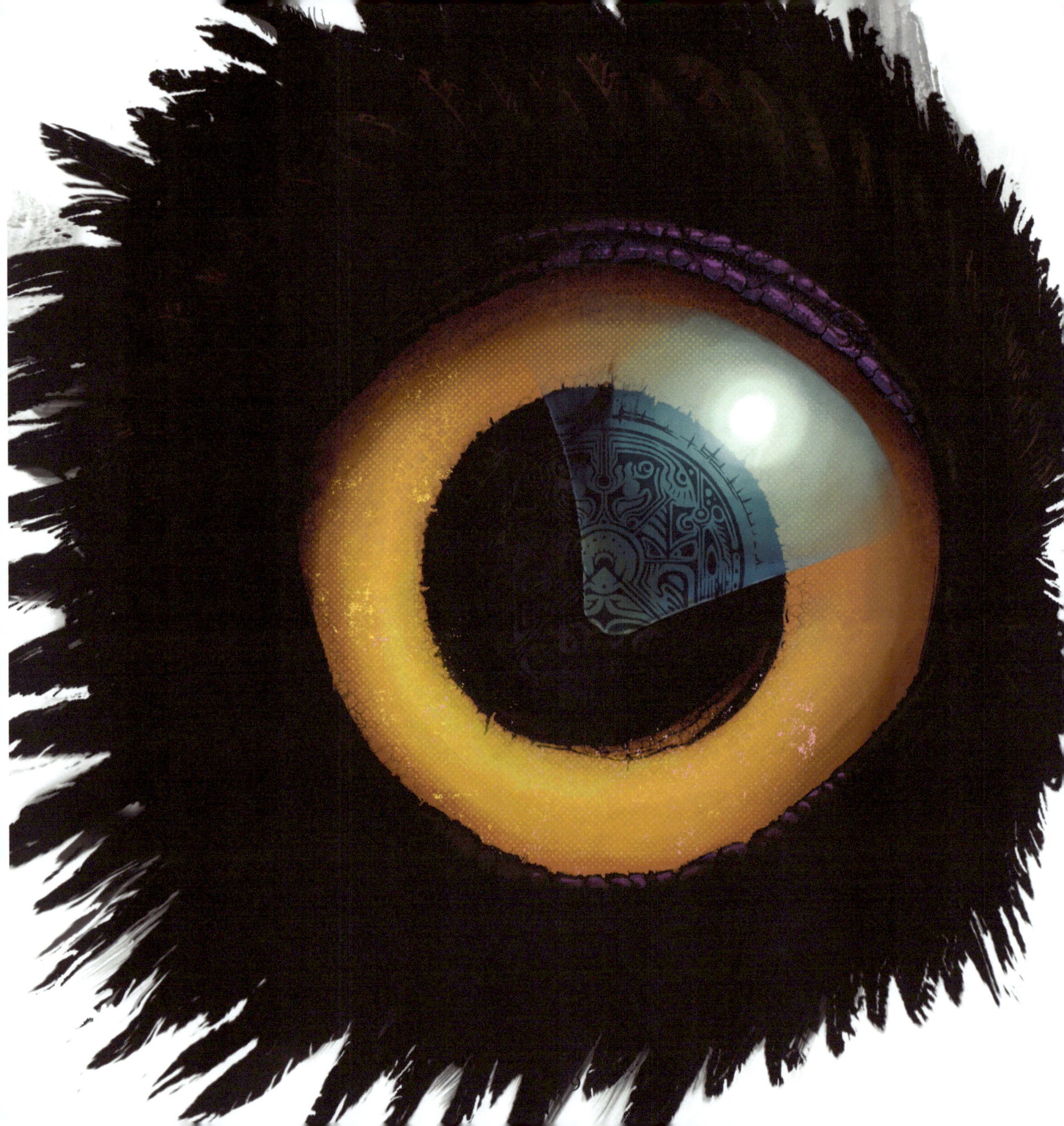

CORVUS JOYOUS

My murder comes on the air.
Cawing.
Shards of letters drawing
blood, Spittle spewed and shrapnel ink.
Because now is the time of crows.

My murder through piercing wings.
Clawing.
Stealing every shiny dawning
moment, To hoard their coins to bribe the boatmen.
Because now is the time of crows.

My murder returns to me at dusk.
Guffaws!
Into my hand they drop flaws
and secrets, Stolen when the tyrant men were smiling.
Shielded by the fearful now reviling.
Silent resistance guiling.
Observed the observing when they hurt her.
Because we have always been the murder.

And this is the time of crows.

THE GHOSTS OF CHRISTMAS PAST

Christmas Eve. The ruins of the old fylit church were nearly impossible to distinguish from the fog if not for a few sputtering candles highlighting the uneven lines of bricks, chiseled a few times over by nature's persistent fury. The overwhelming haze hadn't lifted in days and the denizens of nearby Elphamos Township regarded their sanctuary with terror. The haggard priest paid the fog little mind though, pausing only momentarily to wipe the accumulated moisture from his brow.

His destination, what remained of Our Lady Sara-e-Kali, sat at an odd angle from the ground. During the night, it had slid from its foundations nearly fifteen feet but had otherwise remained miraculously intact. He passed through the stilted entrance, beneath the ruined statues of other, lesser saints, making his way swiftly from the narthex, across the tangled maze of the sanctuary, and into the ambulatory. Thick roots and branches now covered what had once been evenly-cleaved slate blocks and clean column lines, forcing the solid architecture into dangerous arches along precarious curves.

Hidden behind a small pile of unremarkable stones was what had also once been the door to a confessional. Its small wooden carvings scrubbed off by the corrosive magic of the invading Forest and the varnish already showing signs of equally imminent surrender. A brief backward glance into the unseeing eyes of oblivious icons and he gave the door a shove.

The twisted tunnel, filled with tree roots and the fresh scent of earth, ran from the old confessional and entwined its way through more than twelve feet of rock and rubble, rolling and turning into a macabre labyrinth. From time to time, strange chalk drawings of a wheel balanced on the point of an uneven triangle marked a turn or adorned a slight flaw in the walls. The priest kept moving, because the pain in his side was quickly becoming untenable. When his hand came forward to steady his steps, it came away from the wall slick and warm. He glanced down with the first signs of worry; it was a lot of blood.

The priest let out a sound almost like a growl; he had been hit worse than he thought. The shrieking fiends with their switch grass-hide hounds, now long since having vanished into the infernal fog, had caught him before he had meant them to. He'd barely survived the onslaught. Regardless, the man suppressed a chill and kept moving until the fallen remnants of the chancel were in view. Safe once more, or, for now.

Blessedly, within the hour, the hearth fire on the far side of the chamber, which had once also served as a church office, was giving a welcome glow to the cold stones. The carefully applied herbs to his side crunched and crinkled when he moved, but the priest finally sat back without a wince. The pain was nearly gone. With a sigh, he tilted his head to examine the small rolls of paper spread out on the table before him. They were spattered in blood and soil but were still readable and for that he thanked The Lady again.

The room was silent all but for a heavy wooden clock, ticking the hours of their protective barriers away all the while melting into the corner. Soon, the Forest would take that too, molding its sturdy boards and spinning gears into a chaotic image of its former self.

It would come alive in their midst to try and steal away their elders or their children with all the unfeeling cruelty of time that had been stowed away in the beat of its backwards pendulum. For a moment, he thought he could see veiny roots grasping the weights and pulling them back and forth like a game of tug-of-war, but he had no spare moments to think more on it.

Glancing back, he slowly unfurled the first of the rolls, laying each of them out carefully in turn. It was a letter, or at least, what remained of one. He squinted in the dim light trying to make out the scrawl on the ruined paper.

Dear Leaf, Dear Patrin, it began. My dearest Ghost,

By now you have seen to it that Rhuderham's confession will not have repercussions for us in the foreseeable future. Thank you. I simply cannot tolerate any more of these ingrates who have come to think that their salvation must lie in submission to The Forest, if only they are willing to drag everyone else down with them. Faerie grows restless. The Township doesn't have much time before The Forest swallows everything into this fog of confusion. We must act before it is too late. Already the church is almost consumed and when it is gone, no one is safe. We must find the track of the Wheel and leave before no one is left.

Your love,
Synette

The Wheel. The Great Wheel. The bits of parchment on the table began to flutter in an unseen draft. It was their only hope, their last chance, and their greatest fear. No one walked in the Forest except those who did so under its protection. No road was safe but for the one that bore its grooves. The Great Wheel that turned with terrible power and whenever it did, a din of screams would rise up all around it. But as it turned, endless death came to those who fell beneath, followed by life-giving renewal in ordered steps emerging on the other side.

It consumed pandemonium and spun out only patterns, neat and precise. Beautiful compositions of structure and meaning from The Forest's dice rolls of gleeful disorder. Nothing truly born of chaos could approach it. Not even The Forest itself, in truth. And so, many of the peoples of Elphamos had already fled in search of it. With nothing but hope that they might make their new homes in the center of its steadily turning eye.

But to Ghost, it was all just another fairy tale. Stories worn smooth by ages of telling and re-telling, distinct in their message but mutable; each storyteller crafting a different tale such as it would suit them. They were all the same to him. Some ordinary world or another, inhabited by mundane people in the midst of everyday affairs. Animals talking, trolls lurking beneath bridges, and witches frosting their gingerbread houses.

Nimble girls spinning straw into gold, clever children confounding their captors, and people transforming into fish and birds and objects and then back again. Boring, repetitive, triumph where virtue was rewarded, evil was punished, the weak were upheld, and the youngest turned into vanquishers. But fairy tales weren't meant to be this way. And for that reason, he had little hope left. Because these tales actually held warnings for the foolish and lessons for children about the rules they must all abide by.

Their treaty with the Fey Realm was done. Someone, somewhere, had forgotten the dangers of promises broken and discarded under autumn leaves. Forgotten the perils that lurk in dark places where there are no formalities, only woodlice. It was then that the stories returned, tangled together in perverse rhymes.

Now, there was no escape. Their land had been thoroughly stolen by shadows they thought their ancestors had chased back into the sea. But shadows, they learned, don't run. They are invited in at the same time one lights the lamps of welcome. With the fires alight, the Forest had come back and Elphamos, the last echo of a mortal dream, was doomed.

A CLOAK ON THE WAVES

Witch Warden. It wasn't just her name anymore; it was a title that encompassed everything and anything that meant something to her. Ever since she had first faced the summoners in the woods, it had been the sole signifier of a woman once called Synette.

It was late. In the distance, the Township's torch lights tinged the sky a pale teal, sending fickle bursts of soot down to sully those huddling below. She was having that dream again. It was the dream where the world wasn't an endless heartbreak of underground tunnels, of hiding while shivering in the mud. She dreamed that the Wide Eyes and Wish Aways, and their march of The Forest, had lost that fateful day so many forgotten years ago.

She dreamed that all her people had fought valiantly against the invading rot and, though suffering great losses, had emerged victorious. She still sometimes imagined them slashing The Forest trees to tinder, and that they didn't lie dusty and dead in the cracks and crevices of what was once a shining frontier. But that's not how it had gone. The once great boroughs had been wiped out by the first eruptions of the trees.

The Forest had swallowed them whole as they ran...as each world had ended in a single weary stumble. A fairy tale world where gossamer wings blew out like flash paper and laughter had been hidden inside of bells with their clappers cut out. The nightmares won, leaving the rest of the silent apocalypse in their wake. Night after night, this was how she slept.

Witch Warden rose from her pallet and cracked her neck. She couldn't imagine that she was that old but already her bones ached. She surveyed the crumbling underground room that had been her home going on four years. No more than a rat, she would die here with the rest of them. It was alright, she had once thought, at least she would die unbound. After the destruction of her kumpania though, everything had changed.

Those who survived took refuge in the Elphamos Townships, where houses appeared and disappeared on the whims of storms, and those who didn't make it in time were lost to the Forest. The trees had taken everyone they could reach, killed those they couldn't, and had strewn copper pots and horses like discarded toys along the sides of the road. Those who fought back were the first to go. After that, there were no more heroes, only survivors. But they didn't find her, no, not her and not the Underground of Saint Sara by the Sea. Black Sara, Sara Who Went into the Waves, their guardian wandering just as lost as they were.

It was the magic in the end that had truly saved them though. Synette hadn't been a hero, not really. But she knew the magic, gleaned and learned from repeated parables and spoiled books every time she could get one of the fairy summoners to teach her about their ways. In the days following the attacks, as she was swept away with the others — the frightened and the trembling — she had seen the source of that magic. It had to be! As they passed the heaps of the dead and witnessed the rest vanishing into the trees, they had glimpsed something beyond that could tear The Forest out by its very roots.

It looked like a massive metal wheel with a hundred spokes, turning and grinding and rolling along. Vines would grab onto it and be ripped cleanly from the ground. Underbrush would try to take hold only to be crushed underneath it. This was unknown sorcery! Not the magic the fae wielded with the impunity of their natures, but something else.

Something …human? All those who saw it descend would gape in awe at the unrelenting power of the Great Wheel as it passed through. The rest would sketch its effigy onto every surface they could, in the hope of being granted just the smallest spark of its indifferent grace.

For its grace, she had then escaped, running across the chasms and bogs, through the groves and into the barrens. When the fiends came pouring out and the warriors marched on the rousties who resisted, her understanding of the magic had kept her safe. The many secrets, and the bag of trinket tools she had kept, now kept her. Witch Warden remembered the tear-filled days and sweat-soaked nights as she crawled through the ashes in search of succor, only weak spells on faded booklets to sustain her. To the very moment she now opened her eyes, a stronger, older, harder magus.

Saint Sara's Underground had been her home since she had errored into them shortly after the cataclysm. They were all that was left of the resistance, the last remaining changelings against a fey-alien world that was quickly overcoming them. They were battered, all of them; some weak, some strong, some an enigma, others as plain as any other townsfolk.

Twisted lips and shattered horns abounded; blue skin bruised green and pointed ears cut straight down to the lobe. White hair still stained silver and fingerprints left on clothes in permanent red oil. Together, they were all that each other had. They were not fighters; they were just all that was left after the rain had washed the blood from the leaves.

A crackle of energy from the doorway snapped Witch Warden from her reverie. Something was disturbing the wired-up runes from the walkway, the magic calling out in alarm. She moved deftly to her feet and flicked a practiced wrist toward the far wall. Obediently, the oddly shaped iron wand, the one with the crescent moon at its tip, resting on a ramshackle shelf leapt from its perch to her waiting hands.

"Speak and best make it fast." She snarled into the darkness there.

An answering hiss, familiar in its low tone, tugged a smile to her lips.

"It is I, Warden. Move with care." The maimed dwarf hobbled into view.

Witch Warden smiled, "Hello Gormaugh. What brings you this far down the tunnels? I thought you and Andry were hunting for hart tonight." The wand was carefully lowered to her side, lest the skittish man grow more restless.

The small creature tensed at the mention of the mossycoat shapeshifter, another member of the Underground he had often been paired with for hunts. "You know damn well he's never around when he should be, poking his head into this stump or that mushroom ring. Gonna get it lopped off one of these days."

Witch Warden chuckled, gracing the dwarf with one of her infamous raised eyebrows. "I doubt that Gormaugh. Besides, even if he does bring his own trouble, it isn't like he can't just roll up, fold in, and look like anyone or anything within half the reach."

Gormaugh merely grunted his reply. "They'll be back soon; you'd better hurry up." With that and no backward glance, he waddled unsteadily back down the tunnel.

With a careless turn, she ran her hand through unruly locks of bedraggled red hair. She hadn't bothered to cut it in a few years now, and so it fell in unkempt tangles down her shoulders and nearly to her waist. Maybe she'd color it over one of these days.

Something obnoxious, like pink.

Synette grabbed the threadbare witches' hat from the pallet, as it was never far from her hands or her head. The hat, her personal icon and the last memorial of the revered West Wood Witch was the symbol of a hero who had fallen in combat defending Elphamos in the early days. All those who dared call themselves 'witch' paid such homage to her memory and Witch Warden, the keeper of the Underground, bore it as her badge of station. No one would ever forget the final sacrifice of the Witches, the saviors of the last of them.

The main hall: little more than a large open tunnel space, was already packed with chattering fae-kind. Six hours ago, Witch Warden had sent two rousties out onto the surface to retrieve a Circle Scroll, one of the few original maps with known locations of the Wheel. They had gotten word that such a scroll had been hidden in a destroyed archive and, somewhere in the bowels of a ruined book-hoard, may yet survive.

Amergin, an irrepressible animal-speaker, and Liam, a fifteen-year-old fancying himself a hill-born sharpshooter, were due back at any moment. The excitement in the air was palpable as Witch Warden strode in to quickly hushing whispers and giddy smiles through crooked teeth.

The happiness didn't last long though, but then again, it never did anymore. A cry echoed down the causeway and the room fell silent.

No. Not again.

Several of the gathered began to fidget as the scent of blood wafted into the room. It was Amergin who came first, his torn body shaking. Over his small shoulders was draped the remnants of what was Liam. The young boy's gnarled form bleeding from a massive wound to the chest.

Witch Warden barely heard the roustie as the words began to tumble out of his mouth. They had been seen; a troll had caught them unawares as they passed from a ruined wall to a foundation block at a corner where four numbers had been carved into the concrete.

Whatever it was that Amergin said next though, it didn't matter. She knew what had happened. The Forest had already overtaken the cornerstone at the graveyard fence.

Sobs began to choke out into the air followed by a soft, keening sound that grew louder and louder. Somewhere, in her own mind, Witch Warden felt her soul hold desperately to its final breath. Because the eyes that rose from beneath the black brim were clouded with hate and scorched the room.

Without a word of comfort, she took several long strides into the center of the gathering.

"Good night, Liam." Her grim voice chilled those around her. "I'm so sorry."

She stretched the heavy moon wand out from her hand over the still form of the boy.

"Magna res est vocis et silentii temperamentum, Male parta male dilabuntur, Malum quidem nullum esse sine aliquo bono. Frusta per partes, revertere."

As the horrified crowd of otherkin watched in silence and in sorrow, Liam convulsed once, and then again. His eyes fluttered open but it was obvious to all, he saw nothing. His mouth quirked, but not in the sly mischievous way they had all known him for.

The body rose, shambling, coughing, dead still though it moved. The joints popped until they could lurch mechanically, and his spine seemed to swivel as if hung from an unholy hoist latch, whose ring had not been sufficiently greased.

Witch Warden lowered the wand and gazed into the face of the dead automaton. For a moment, her eyes then flicked to the faces of those gathered around her.

"This changes nothing." Her voice was cold, near heartless. "You know the way, Liam. We need that map, or we all perish here and now. Bring me the Scroll." She raised her hand and pointed a sharp finger toward the causeway. "You heard me." Her voice rose, wavering slightly. "Go!"

The corpse shambled past the silent group, bent once more to the task at hand, but no longer with a chewed lip or a nervous quip. That would never happen again. In fact, there went the boy who had been trying to write their stories, to record their losses. He'd tried poetry to make sense of the overwhelming emptiness.

But his journal was mostly filled with half-formed phrases and nonsensical lyrics, the ink dripped into puddles on the edge of the paper when he could no longer see through the tears. On the first page of his journal, next to a crude double circle, he'd written, 'It is the oldest shape revered, found not made, persevered. Everywhere in time and space, spiral chased in perfect place. Too precise, they worry, to be nature. Too profound, they say, to be man.'

The eyes of the Underground turned to the Witch Warden as she stood at their center in silence, watching the dead man return to his appointed purpose. There was sadness there, but the face of the Warden would not break, would not betray a heart that may as well have stopped beating with Liam's that very same moment. No one seemed to doubt the necessity of her actions, but they could not yet reconcile within themselves that none had been willing to actually do what she had done.

Witch Warden turned and walked effortlessly back into the tunnel, back to her sanctuary in the depths of a root cellar. In the secret space of the little room, late into the night, Synette wept, her tears falling onto the grooves of a Grand Wheel etched into the stone. Filling it, until they poured down to the ground through the concentric circles underneath it.

Before dawn, she pulled out a scrap of paper and summoned a crow. Dear Ghost, it began. The time has come...

FAIRLY WAYFARING

I thought that it was just a scarecrow, if not for the line of footprints that trailed behind it. He had walked, alone, through thick mud the night before; now dried into a stumbling rut of weed-stamped footprints. He, or maybe it, was also standing out in a horse pasture, knee-deep in alfalfa that wasn't, as crops go, at all concerned with flocks of birds. So, like any lost scarecrow, he stuck out on the open plain just as much as a broken stump might.

When I got to him, though, I wasn't sure what I was looking at. A young man, but only maybe. His feet still and steady underneath him but his back bent at the waist so that his arms dangled loosely over his sides. In his unmoving hand was a crescent wrench and I could not believe what he had done with it.

Four bolts held a piece of broken metal in the shape of an elephant's head to his face, screwed right into his skull. A dusty car hose then connected the middle of his head into a trunk that wrapped around his torso twice before it was secured by wire to his hip. A strange collar of bells, cobbled together from various windchimes and cut-up lawn ornaments, was wrapped around his neck.

Far too tight to be good for him. But the most disturbing thing of all was his arms and hands. The exposed flesh around them was clearly greenish and moldy, but the bones appeared to have turned to iron rods, joints soldered with rainbow-like lead. He was exactly like all those old wives tales and scary stories people used to tell around campfires; where a particularly gruesome looking scarecrow actually turns out to be an abandoned corpse.

I didn't dare touch him, but I tried to call out. I tried to ask if he was alright. But the figure didn't move. It only seemed to be pointing at a large slot in a metal plate nailed to his chest. I recognized the plate, weirdly enough. It was an old, ornate, coin door from an arcade cabinet. Or was it a gumball machine? One cent embossed on either side of two key-back cranks.

What else could I do but stand there, frozen in confusion and terror. Whatever this zombie-marionette was, it had come from the woods a half-mile beyond and had just somehow stopped here. Unable to move any further, I suspected, because it had run out of pennies. So, I left it there and ran. I ran all the way back to the caravan and babbled away about what I had seen.

My name, if you must know, is Amos, except of course, that it isn't. The Ringmaster calls me Amos. It was the name of the township I came from before I ran away to join the circus. It was the best I could do since my father had died a wheat farmer. It was the wheat that killed him. He had gone out one morning because something was leaving trails in the field, crushing twisting lines through the best stalks. He followed those trails and never returned; at least, not until his body turned up in a ditch a year later.

Eaten by wolves, the police said. But there were no wolves, and everyone knew it. Rather, for the last few seasons that I can remember in Amos Town, he had argued with our neighbor, Evan Pritchard. Our community was small, smaller than most, and land was always in argument. But when people argue, they get mad, and then they make mistakes.

After two rounds of conflict over less than a yard, my father was the first to make that mistake. In the spring of that year he planted, not four feet too far to the left onto Pritchard land, but four feet too far to the right, past the boundary that marked the beginning of the forest. The leaf litter was barely noticeable, so I suppose that's why he didn't see it. But that simple mistake would eventually be the end of old Amos Senior.

The fae that first appeared didn't trouble us until harvest, when the most prosperous crop my father had ever seen, was ready for the threshing floor.

He was Old Jack Sprat, he said. This short, ugly thing in an orange hat and green pants puffed out with straw. Underneath you could see that he was a skeletal man whose clothes had been made opulently plump by stuffing them with dried herbs that smelled of lavender or, possibly lemon balm.

"I am old Jack Sprat!" He said, and he said it exactly like that. "I am the bridegroom come. I'll choose a bride, a goodly girl, and not one small as a crumb. From the church, she'll get a fine horse to ride, and if no mare will take her; then prepare me a wheelbarrow for this lane, to spur us on 'til flowers o'er take 'ere!"

In return for the bounty of faerie soil, Jack Sprat was demanding a tax on our harvest and a wife, chosen from a few marriageable girls. The Township panicked, the faerie wheat was surely tainted anyway, and no one would buy any from my father, but even more so, no one was going to be giving up a daughter for the folly of one cantankerous farmer.

So, while Jack Sprat's offer was hard to swallow, it was also steep enough to mean the risk of starvation for all my brothers and sisters, my aunts and uncles, and everyone else. But it didn't matter anyway. My father refused to tithe. That's why when he went out to shoo off whatever it was that kept damaging the wheat he was about to cut, the wheat threshed and ate him.

Too bad it didn't satisfy the Geas though. Some ancient taboo from our ancestors had been broken and now that Jack Sprat had been denied his fair due, Amos Township was also doomed. The church grounds were the first to be taken by the forest. One misty morning, roots and branches burst out from what was once solid stone and mortar, erupting from graves where they had fed on faithless bones and coffins for centuries beyond remembering. The main lane and the bridge were the next to follow.

We all ran, clumping together on the road hoping to find a place still safe to rest. But the Stopping Places had moved along with The Forest, and we couldn't remember where to find them anymore. That's sort of how I ended up standing in a pasture, face to face with a revenant who had been rebuilding himself from scavenged car parts and abandoned appliances while he walked in decay.

The last of us had joined up with a traveling carnival show, always moving from place to place. Mostly because plenty of towns wanted us, but no one would actually have us. We could make them laugh, but best be gone before they frown, you know? So, right now, we were between crossing signs, and I thought I had seen someone coming towards us from the road.

To my relief, no matter what outlandish things I said, everyone in the carnival believed me. Even Sigmar, the fish keeper, nodded in grave understanding. He too had once run afoul of the fae and had broken a promise to the Pond Prince out of youthful ignorance.

"Colors only fire can destroy, colors only fire can impart," he'd say cryptically. "Saw a mermaid in the river, but it was really a giant carp."

Now, he carried bowls of small grey goldfish wherever he went. He was adamant that they could only be "liberated" in an elaborate trial he'd set up as a midway game for funfair visitors. It involved throwing a ping-pong ball into the tops of their glass jars. A yellow ball meant that the player got to keep the goldfish. A blue ball meant that they got three extra yellow balls for free. But those fish who got the red ball in their waters were then wrapped in paper and condemned to death by being thrown to the crows.

"Out there, in the field!" I gasped. "I don't know what it is, but I think someone, someone strange is coming. He looks like a mannequin, or, uh, a machine! He's not right!"

Our Ringmaster, the venerable old tinsmith Enda Aodh, pushed the brim of his hat up and stared quietly out into the field. Without a word, he reached up to the scarf around his neck and gave me two silver coins plucked from the jingling fringe. He nodded towards the figure, and the entire caravan waited.

"Well, go on, boy. Take the message and send'm on back."

I must have stared in oblivious horror for too long because eventually, I got a boot in the backside. Even so, I couldn't manage more than a slow shuffle out to into the long grass until I finally wandered back up to...whatever he was. I held the coins out in my hand, but he didn't move. I stepped closer and waved my palm under his extended finger. Nothing. So, finally, with a nervous giggle I couldn't stifle, I leaned over as far as I could and plugged the two coins into the slot. Still nothing.

I stared at the crank on his chest plate with a scowl of disgust. I regretted even mentioning this strange abomination at all and vowed that the next time I saw something truly out of the ordinary, I was going to ignore it. You don't have to do creepy things if you never talk to the creepy monsters. Now that was real wisdom!

I turned the key-crank; once, twice, maybe thrice until I heard it click. Then, I very nearly fell straight over, arms flailing, when a little card suddenly popped out of the elephant's mouth. It was a little sticky and made from old paperstock, like what they used to print playing cards on, and it read: "Meet us at the ring of crows," hand-written in cursive blue ink.

That was it, I turned right around and ran for the safety of the road. But then again, I think the old scarecrow did exactly the same thing. All I could hear was the sound of grinding gears and misaligned joints fading away between the trees.

THE WAY BY AND BY THE WAY

She watched him with great interest, as she usually did. But Ghost was completely engrossed with his examination of Liam's mystical transformation. Witch Warden was pleased that the crescent wand had done its good work, but why the deathly boy now appeared in the guise of a circus elephant was anyone's guess. Or, as much as he had managed to interpret a circus elephant with debris stolen from the ditches of protesting corvids.

Ghost, who had gotten the nickname from the unusually pale coloration of his hair and eyes, pushed the sleeves of his ruined cassock past his elbows and began to tinker with some of the finer widgets that had grown in place of fingernails, hair, and teeth. In fact, the boy seemed to have managed to replace almost every part of himself in less than a day, save for the muscles of his arms and the contents of his ribs and spine. Even his joints were mostly cobbled together out of bolted hinges at this point, and his blood looked like an oil slick.

"Astounding." Ghost stated. "I've never seen the magic work like this before. How did you do it?"

"I'm not sure I did, to be honest." She replied. "Strange as it is to say, I think this is Liam's doing. He went out, dead like the others, but built this all himself. This.... armor. His mind must have survived enough of the The Forest to become, I don't know how else to say it, but some kind of mechanical knight. A Stumble Errant, if there is such a thing."

"With an elephant's face?"

"You know, if I had to guess, I'd bet he got that from an old Elephant and Castle pub sign. Must have found one discarded out in a trash heap."

"Elephant and Castle?"

"Yeah, it goes back to the Guilds. Medieval Guilds, you know? The Worshipful Company of Cutlers, who used to make swords and knives with ivory handles. Their symbol was an elephant carrying a castle on its back. I'm surprised to see that there are any people out there who still remember them. Much less to mark establishments with their heraldry."

Ghost pinched his forehead. "Why would Liam choose such a thing? With a bell collar and all this...this...junk?"

Thoughtfully composed, Witch Warden stepped over to the serene automaton and knocked against the hard brass plate welded to his chest. The soft clink of something inside piqued her interest but it was Ghost who cautiously unlatched the door, catching two small coins with his hand as they rolled out.

Synette smiled as she saw an icon of a hare on one side and a horse on the other. "Travellers." She breathed, hints of shock and excitement in her tone. "He must have gone ooking for the Travellers. And found them I'd say!"

Ghost still seemed perturbed, mostly out of confusion. Witch Warden explained. "An lucht siúil Mincéirí. The Walking People. Humans, who circle the outermost boundaries of the Way By. Probably some of the last descendants of those who made their bargains with the Oldest Ones. They took with them many words of the Way and made the Shelta speak to hide our secrets. Then, they mixed it with Hindi and English tongues to dress it respectably. They are a jumble, a hodgepodge. Mosaics, mishmash, and mergings of all kinds. In and out and in between. They are By the Way."

"By the Way." Ghost repeated to himself as he turned the coins over across his knuckles. "But if Liam found Travellers By the Way, then this is a caravan that should have crossed at least once before. Do you think they could…"

"…cross us back us out?" She finished, pleased with her turn of phrase.

Ghost looked up with the barest hint of hope and the Witch Warden laid an affectionate palm against his cheek. "Stumble Liam seems to think so, and I agree. We gather everyone up and take the coins to the river. If the Great Wheel is with us, we'll both come 'round again."

"And if not, we blaspheme the night with our blood and are massacred in The Forest."

"We're all going to die when it gets here anyway, and you know that. It spreads by the minute. We have no choice, my summer shade, we have to leave. Shed our tears, yes. But leave. This was our home. It's not anymore. We are our home now and it travels with us until we find somewhere to set it down again."

Ghost felt his fingers close over the thin metal. He knew she was right. By the Way, it was their only chance.

The gathered Township of Elphamos was fewer in number than ever before. Hunched in the moldering pews of the church, they listened with anxious disquiet as Witch Warden set out their path. For the moment, the menacing trees were slowed as they grew fat on the soil of the burial ground.

The church cemetery, whose most recent grave was the only one that could be read the same upside or down: 1888, was now filled to bursting with the weald. This meant that the safest tunnels would take them east towards the river. Always they would need to keep the sound of snapping branches behind them and the babble of the water before them. Many were injured and frightened, but all were resigned.

The Ghost and the Witch Warden had never led them astray and as they had each faced The Forest at least once in their travels, they knew that anyone left behind would never be seen again. Run or perish. Both options were equally luckless of course, but now the sheltering fae of Elphamos finally understood the true difference between those who made bad choices and those who only had bad choices.

They passed silently into the burrows beneath the old fields less than an hour later. The group was sluggish, so as to be quiet and careful. Every now and again the roots groaned as they slipped by, or the air would suddenly taste of dry ash. In the Way By, every stone had a name, and every hewn wall could speak. Steps had to be composed like music, to lull the crushed peat moss back to sleep.

Ghost remained at the head of the line, Witch Warden at the rear. Her iron wrench poised to take on anything that might think to ambush them in the darkness. They each also kept one of Liam's coins, while Liam himself faltered unsteadily in the middle. Synette had placed his journal in the rib-space behind his coin slots, and he could feel the pages tearing into little strips as the book knocked back and forth in his gears. One of the torn slips popped out with a whirr and a clunk when he accidentally stubbed his foot on a buried rock.

The uileann piper behind him snatched it out and squinted in the dim light. "It says, 'Throw a penny in the fountain and make a wish.'" He read. "What does that mean?"

"It means we make for the river as planned." Ghost answered. Dabbling his fingers in the air with a cryptic flourish, "I think I might even know of what penny he speaks."

Witch Warden then simply spurred them on, the sound of encroaching thickets starting to worry her.

But to her relief, they all arrived at the mouth of an old cistern not long after, one that had not been once packed with the dead during earlier centuries of plague and drought. The river beyond thus ran clean and shallow, tumbling over rocks and somersaulting through pond lilies with the carefree joy of reunited raindrops.

"This is it." Ghost announced, pulling a silver coin from the pocket in his sash. He balanced it on his thumb and turned to the bedraggled company. "Make a wish." He said blithely, before pausing a second or two and flipping the piece into the water.

A small child with hawk's feet looked weirdly saddened at the loss of the coin. "Why do we do that?" He asked abruptly, as the coin immediately dropped into the silt. Ghost turned, "Why do we throw the coins in the water? The coin toss has always been sacred to us, Miri."

"Yes, but I thought that was just for luck. We came out here for that?"

"People who walk beside rivers know that water cleanses and water kills. It brings prosperity but drowns the unwary. Most importantly though, it can also lead you to others, to refuge, when you are lost in the wild. In ancient times, we would throw in a beautiful stone, then it became a figure of clay, or something whittled in bone. Then coins came with symbols printed right on them for the exchanges of empires, and we threw them in to show that the water still has authority over even the highest kings. Settled folk now say we just 'follow the money,' and they mean this with cruelty. But we follow the money because we give it in the hopes of receiving the boons of such sacrifices. Of being brought back into harmony with those around us. Because our coins only work to bind us if we trust each other."

"Look!" Amergin nearly shouted. "It's going that way, against the stream!"

"Everyone, quickly now!" Witch Warden plead. "Follow it! Follow the glint in the water and don't lose sight of it!"

Several of the Elphamos families picked up their children immediately and took off at a steady jog. Others helped the elder members by lifting them onto their backs or cradling them in their four to six arms, moving slower but keeping a keen sight of those ahead. Ghost nodded to Witch Warden and joined the second group, lending what strength he could to keep pace with the tiny, almost willow-wispy, light as it bounced along the trail.

Witch Warden, on the other hand, turned to Liam. His mechanics were attached too awkwardly for him to run, and he was far too heavy for her to carry. Yet, the rules of Elphamos had always been exacting, and if they now carried Elphamos with them, the rules would still have to be honored. He could not be left behind.

She raised the iron wand once more and worked its complicated magic from the exposed point of his hip to his backwards-facing knee. In short order, when she had detached his torso from his legs, she raised gentle Liam onto her shoulders and pulled his suspenders around her arms to keep him hoisted high. He'd have to face backwards unfortunately, since the key cranks of his metal door stuck out too far for comfort. But without any sign of protest, she thought she saw something beneath the elephant mask smile or wink. A card spit out with a gurgling cough and lingered in the air in time for her to catch it.

A Penny Saved is a Penny Earned

Synette shook her head, sighed, and started off at a trot. "Don't worry." She said to the rattling automaton. Her voice almost verging on sarcasm as she responded. "We'll catch it."

SALT OF THE EARTH

"Amos."

Yeah, I heard it. I just didn't want to.

"Amos!" The Ringmaster snapped. He knew I could hear him too.

"Yes, sir?" I grumbled. The day was already getting uncomfortably hot, and it wasn't even noon. The sun seemed determined to make every minute more agonizing than the last and all I wanted to do was hide under a tree. But Old Enda Aodh had, for some reason, taken us out into the absolute prairie. There wasn't an overhanging tree within two miles in any direction and here he demanded we pitch the Big Top. And let me say, as tents go, this one was a canopy with enough shade for a hundred and twenty feet worth of spectators. But until those rainbow banners were streaming, it was nothing but a mangled pile of stakes, ropes, and metal rods.

I picked up one of the large side panels and made some demonstration of examining the stitching. The panel had a huge canvas painting on it, as they all did, of some famous sideshow performer from the past.

People most often called them 'freaks' back then and many still do but we used the portraits to remember those who had come before us and who had built this community. This one was "The Elephant Man," Joseph Merrick. Everyone had done him wrong; everyone in his life and then in his death too. But we still remember him from the stories passed down through the caravans of the Leicester Unparish. Apparently, he loved to dance at the penny gaff shows and had quite the performer's wit.

"Imagine what that would have been like." It was Greater Katie Contour, the contortionist. "Being carnie back then. Everyone come to gawk at you whether you like it or not, and figuring that at least you'd get some coins out of them for a decent supper later. And if you didn't look the part, you'd have to slide an icepick up your nose or eat fire. Or someone keeps you in a cage, like the animals. No difference, I guess. Carnie people and carnie animals were the same thing to settled folks. Joseph, they call the Elephant Man. Like he was Jumbo or something, you know?"

"Jumbo?" I asked. She looked back at me with an expression of pity.

"Biggest circus elephant who ever lived. Higher'n ten feet. Quite the shock back in the 1800s, you know. No one around here saw elephants in those days and certainly not elephants that big. Died when he got hit by a train though. So, they cut his body up into pieces and sold it off for exhibits." She touched the painting with gentle fingers. "Joseph too. See?"

I shrugged uncomfortably before continuing to unroll the tent sections. "Yeah, I guess."

"Hey!" She snapped, grabbing my wrist. "Amos! Watch out!"

I stopped and, I admit, stared at her blankly. All I could see was a sea of peeling paint and a lot of work ahead of me.

Greater Katie pointed at the ground near my feet with a stern pout. Carefully, I followed her gaze and glanced down, expecting to be a step away from some venomous snake or something. But instead, it was just a dead bird. Tiny, and already woven by decay into the long grass. I turned back to her, my lip hanging open, and blinked.

She sighed, deeply and intentionally. "Gods, Amos, don't you know anythin'!? Look at it. It's a nestlin' bird, a fortnight old at the most. Fell from the nest and was gone. Its parents never even noticin' an absence in the chirp, chirp, chirp. See how small, how delicate. Skin just paper thin. It'll rot out to nothin' in less time than it took to hatch. No name. No colors. It barely lived and will not be remembered. Because it was never known. By birds, by sun, or by people hearin' its song."

Katie Contour had always had a poetic bent to her speech, developed over years of carnival barking, but this was more than I was used to.

"You look away and pay no attention," she shook her finger at my nose. "And then you'll step on it. Never, ever, step on it. That's when you stumble."

With that, she huffed and stalked away, as if she'd imparted some kind of common knowledge that everyone knew but me. I didn't even have time to point out to her that there were no trees out here. So where could a twelve-day-old hatchling-bird even come from? And stumble? So what?

All the same, we raised the Big Top that afternoon and chatted about the horse fairs. It was hours of hoisting and losing metal screws in the dirt. I did stay away from the bird though, just in case. When the main pavilion was up and washed, Enda finally came around to inspect our work. He checked that the portrait panels were all in the right order, that the rings inside were marked, and that our camp was positioned far enough away that the lights of our wagons wouldn't interfere with the lights of the fair.

I watched him go through his usual rounds, blue and purple lanterns speckling his jacket like butterfly wings in a flower patch, as I picked beans and sprouts from my tin cup, chewing the sweet brown sugar as slowly as possible. Randomly, I found myself wondering if fairy was actually supposed to be another word for carnie. If a person from the carnival was a carnie, then a person from the fair must be a fairie. Right? But what would be the difference? Well, our old Ringmaster sure looked like a bit of both right then.

"Amos."

Yeah, I heard it. I just didn't want to. So, I rolled back over in my blankets and ignored the sound.

"Amos!" The Ringmaster snapped. Now, of course, he knew I could hear him too.

"Yes, sir?" I grumbled; my eyes crusted with sleep.

"Get up, boy. It's time."

I raised my head only a fraction of the way off my pillow. "It's dark out there. Middle of the night, Enda. What's the problem?"

He kicked the boards that protected my cozy little nest. "Fine, fine." I said. "I'm coming already. Storm comin'? Tent fall over or what?"

But that wasn't it at all. When I finally crawled out from under the bed, everyone was already gathered by the campfire. They looked nervous, some maybe even excited. But a lot of them kept glancing at me and then looking away again.

"What's going on?" I asked. Junk Germaine, our best roustabout and all-around scavenger of useful things, pulled me over to his side. "Surprised you don't remember this old place." He joked. "S'where we picked you up."

I tried to take the whole of the landscape in, even dark and blue in the midnight hour. Tall grasses hissed softly in the wind, the wide-open sky twinkled with its own Big Top star-lights as cloud banners wicked up the last pinks and oranges from the dewy damp horizon. But no matter how much I tried to focus on the hills and rocks that could have been there years ago, I still didn't recognize this place. I had joined up at the side of the road, or so my memories told me, but I couldn't seem to conjure the field around it.

Junk Germaine slapped my shoulder gleefully. "No worries, Amos. We got'tu. Family always got'tu. But we've come 'round again finally and it's time to pull up the door on that old well."

"Old well." I said, watching in confusion as fireflies from out in the meadows began to bounce into camp.

"No ask why." Junky stopped me. "The why ain't make no sense to nobody anyhow. You'll see. Then you'll know."

CIRCUS OF THE MÉSALLIANCES

An hour we processioned through the field. All in a line, reverently carrying our candles and lamps, as if on a pilgrimage to the sea. Enda Aodh guided our steps in every way; from which direction we turned as we walked to precisely where we could place our feet. I kept glancing back at Greater Katie and thinking about the little dead bird that no one else knew about.

'Don't stumble' she had said to me again, before we left camp. And I was trying desperately not to, even when it felt like the reeds were wrapping around my ankles and trying to trip me. I still didn't recognize anything we passed either, despite Junky's insistence that I had been found here the last time the caravan had taken this route.

Not the old stone fences we climbed over and not the ruins of a church leaning against an oak tree bigger around than history had been long. We kept going until I thought I could hear water running in the distance. It wasn't particularly loud. Like a small stream, maybe. Or the run-off from a hard rain.

When the Ringmaster stopped next to a withered signpost, I was confused. The sign was still pointed, like an arrow, but the nail had rusted so badly that the heavy wood front had tipped forward and so it simply pointed down. There was no writing on it either. Not even an impression where something carved might have worn away.

Enda Aodh surveyed the silent gathering, who all clutched at their lights to prevent the wind from licking them up. He then looked at me before leaning down and clearing years of blown silt from a heavy wooden circle embedded in the ground. It was huge! Made of layered planks easily as old as the church-tree we'd gone by, it could hold four rousties with an inch left over. It took six to move it though.

They dug and heaved, rocking the well-cover back and forth until the mud finally let go of it. The moss clung to the top though, and with its covering of fallen leaves it was a surprise that anyone could have found it at all. But it was when they made the first real progress on moving it that I started to get a strange feeling.

It slid, not very far, but just enough to form a black crescent on the edge of the well. It was too dark both down below and up here to see anything. But, for a second, I thought I heard the echo of voices. The six roughnecks in charge of the chore heaved again, and this time the lid rolled up, turned like a spun coin, and fell flat into the heath. It's a good thing that fescue doesn't really crush. But after that, I don't think my eyes, or my mind, were working very well. Old Enda Aodh walked right up to the edge of that ancient stone circle and reached his hand straight out over the void below.

A moment later, a silver coin popped up from the mouth of the well, as though someone at the bottom had flipped him a sixpence sterling. Then, I realized, it was one of the same coins as he had sent off with the scarecrow, plucked from his own scarf.

That's when they emerged.

The first was a man with skin like an ashen sky, slate blue with white scars around his right eye and slit down his chin. He wore the cassock of a priest, and his hair was long and white, as if he were very old. But as far as I could see, his skin was smooth of any wrinkles and his strength spry. When he saw me, the shape and appearance of his face was exactly like mine. I gasped. I froze. We might as well have been twins.

From there, two women climbed up. One was missing an eye, which she kept in a sea-glass jar tied to her belt. The other had the horns of a goat and armored plates on her shoulders that could have been the backs of giant beetles. I think, then, they pulled up a green-skinned boy with endless black eyes and no discernable nose. A pale girl followed with sharply arched ears and a sickly look. Was that then a gruff little man, wide shoulders, heavy feet, and thick red beard?

After him, all I know is that they just kept coming. More than twenty in all, pulled from the well and happily greeted by my caravan. I think I overheard some of them say how grateful they were to be saved, how long their journey had been to get here, but I still couldn't get my thoughts to properly understand what was going on. Ten minutes ago we had been no more than a ragged group of carnies, found and bound by bonds of burden, and now?

"Wha.... I...." I babbled. "Who are they? Where.... where did they come from?"

The Ringmaster quirked an eyebrow. "From the same place you did, Amos." He stated. "Don't you recognize your, well, shall we say, your other half?" Here he motioned to the man in the cassock. "I suspect he's keen to see you again after all these years."

Enda was right. He was me and I was him. He stood before me with a gentle smile. "They call me Ghost now." He said. "Though, I thank you for your restitution. Without it, Liam would never have been able to help us escape The Forest alive. I've never known a nicer changeling than you, Amos."

This is why I was asking you. Would you have remembered much in my place?

There is nothing else I know until the dawn came. Because I thought I must have been dreaming and even when you just think that you were dreaming something, you start to forget details. Because when I opened my eyes, I was back in my bed, behind the boards of the undercarriage.

Coffee was already on the fire and the smell, mixed with morning-wet peat, was a wish come true. Maybe that's what my fantasies had been about, throwing a penny in a wishing well and getting the strongest brew hearth-magic could make!

But the face that greeted me as I climbed out and back up to my feet was that of a witch in a tall witch's black hat. Her seedy red hair twisted like vines and bloomed into knots almost thick enough to cover everything but her eyes. She pointed a wrench at me with an uncalled-for sneer.

"Amos." She said. "High time you were up and moving. Ghost is waiting for you."

Then, to my stupefaction, she straightened up and returned to fussing over, my gods, it was the scarecrow! Well, half of him anyway.

Some of the other rousties had managed to take the suspension irons off of an old wagon and had fashioned them into the shapes of legs. Springs stuck out oddly and tension rods were in the process of being screwed into place near the mechanical man's hips, but as I watched, still in the dazed space between sleep and awake, I swear that I saw her work magic with that old ratchet. I blinked. Or, at least, I think that I must have blinked, because then the automaton stood up.

Adjusting his elephant-shaped mask slightly, he started to walk. Robotically at first, but then smoother and smoother as his chattering retinue worked out the kinks.

A long morning shadow crossed mine. It was Enda, by the looks of the folded arms and spiked hair.

"Who are they?" I asked. A centaur with a broken foot was arguing with our farrier as he filed an overgrown back hoof held precariously between his knees.

A fae sprite, whose thick braids concealed long sloping horns, rattled a music box before climbing inside it to take the place of the twirling plastic ballerina. Who, for being a poor rendition of a dancer, was chucked unceremoniously into the grass. When another of my company walked past with an armful of acrobat's costumes to be washed, the top garment opined as to its preferred mixture of soap powders.

"Travellers." He said. "Refugees. Belonging nowhere and everywhere, like us. Just trying to find their Way as the Way takes them."

"And...Ghost?"

The old Ringmaster smiled. "You don't remember those days anymore. When we found you. Little imp then, and just as much of an imp now." He shone in a way I had never seen before, and his smile was filled with happy thoughts that darted across his eyes and leapt off the glint of his teeth. "We'd lost so many of our own, thrown so many coins down that well, wishing for the better prosperity of our people. They left you at the edge of a wheat field, they did. Crying your sore little eyes out, babbling on about how the township folks had hid you from the mean Old Jack Sprat. Tricked him good with that trade, I'll tell you. Gave him a shadow, kept the rascal. Too bad he came for our kin, anyway. It's all in the bargain, eh, Amos?"

"You mean..." I trailed off. "We're all..."

AXIS MUNDI

The wheel spokes of a long vardo caravan creaked as they turned in perfect rhythm to a second silver coin skipping gaily down the road. Old Enda Aodh, clad in bright pink and black pinstripes, clicked his horse faster; a sturdy piebald Vanner by the name of Kush. Kush, on the other hand, rather fancied the long green grass on the roadside and kept veering towards the right to see if he could grab a mouthful on the way by. The Ringmaster chided him from the driver's seat. The sun was low, and they had no time to dally.

From inside the house-on-wheels however, Witch Warden was once again working her magic. She strapped and built, tinkered until the tiny gears timed in unison, and then turned to the rest of the salvaged parts with a frown. A new set of brass bolts, welded lead lines holding panes of glass, and a crank-run music box to act as both a chair and a note player.

When the odd-looking display box was complete, one of the palette mixers in the company would paint the outside a bright red with gold and white lettering that read, The Faded Fortune Teller – See Your Future with Liam the Mechanical Wonder! The titular Liam himself sat across from her, his elephant's face expressionless if not for the curious tilt to his head and the way his gaze seemed to follow her from one end of the floor to the other. The wrench twirled in her hand before alighting across the cogs and sparking them into life.

The wheels of the vardo turned over and over beneath her, the wood scraping against upturned stones as they trod forever downward, out of the highest hills and into the valley, following the money. Ghost had flipped the coin over his elbow that morning just as camp had been struck and the fires buried. It had landed on 'heads' and then spun about before jingling off through a barely used trail.

Now, they all counted their paces to keep up; some on foot to maintain a wary eye on the edges of the woods, and others inside to prepare food and mend shoes. They'd been steady on all day and there was no telling if or when they could rest.

So, each of the changelings, fae, fae-kind, or their human counterparts, worked in shifts to keep the other from collapsing. It was uncannily easy, they found, given how familiar each turned out to be to the other. Ghost had chosen to stick to the road though and strode confidently alongside an anxious Amos, who had also decided to press ahead for as long as their destination, wherever it was, took to reach.

"So, are you me, or am I you?" He asked.

Ghost looked askance with a wry smile. "Or am I me and you, are you?"

"We're not supposed to riddle each other, you know? That's for outside the rings."

The man in the flowing black cassock laughed. His emphasis on the last two words had made the question uninterpretable, but one answer could have been just as true as any other.

"You know what I mean. Which of us was first?"

"First? Hardly. We've always been at exactly the same time. What you mean is where."

"Where? Where what?"

"Exactly."

Amos jumped over a fallen branch. "Fine then. Have your head-teasers. But don't go saying you're me. I get into enough trouble as it is and I won't be blamed for what you get up to."

Ghost agreed. "Don't worry. I'll see that our name stays as clean as can be. And I'll light us two candles if I can't."

Amos scowled. "Are you actually a priest then? I...well, you don't seem like much of a priest to be honest."

"That depends on what you think a priest is."

"Um. Someone you confess to?"

"Then I'd say I'm a priest whether I want to be or not."

"But..."

A shout from up ahead drew the entire caravan to a sudden halt. Poised for such a warning, Witch Warden leapt from the back door of the lead wagon and joined Ghost and Amos next to Enda Aodh, who clutched Kush's reins uncertainly.

"What is it?" Witch Warden shouted.

"The coin!" A voice shouted back. "It's stopped!"

Nearly the whole of the procession scurried out onto the gravel, rushing forward to see what, if anything, they could see. But it was Sigmar, the fish keeper, who was the first to point out a shape in the distance. A large, rounded shape concealed by the dusky light.

For all her bluster, Witch Warden could feel tears stinging the corners of her eyes. Could it be? Could it possible, finally, be? She gripped the crescent wand harder in her hand and took a few tentative steps out in front of the gathering crowd. A spell on her lips, she prepared for the worst and prayed for the intervention of Saint Sara.

Somewhere, along the way, they had left the main road, but she could not recall when that had happened. In any case, it was nothing but a flat open moorland ahead of her, with a single copse of trees at its center so utterly out of place one could not help but stare at it. Hoofprints of sheep and shepherds dotted the ground and wandered off towards the silhouette of houses on the far horizon.

She could even once more hear the sound of a river not far from where they all stood. The air was crisp and sweet, ruffling the leaves with a taste of ripe red fruit. If anything in the Book of Genesis was right, this had to be Eden. She was sure of it.

Several of the Travellers immediately went to secure the horses and block the wagons, lest they roll off during their distraction. But all the others, instinctively pressed together for protection, began the slow march out onto the heath. They left the second silver coin as it had fallen, its face merry as it turned towards the grove.

Even Amos was uncharacteristically excited as he high-stepped tussocks in an attempt to ungainly run. What they didn't see was the fallen road sign that the coin had collided with, halting its journey towards the water. Barely legible, with mixed-up chalky writing, it might have read: wilcuman æppelby.

But it was Ghost who finally stopped and breathed deeply of the free galloping winds, sifting through his hair as they did the furrows of the land. He was already in awe of it, his faith in the world above and the world below blooming with renewed vitality.

Before them, beneath years of overgrowth, saturated with lichens, and completely obscured by a boulder surrounded in trees, sat the icon of the never-ending circle. Spokes like that of a vardo. Iron scaffolds like that of a Big Top. Shims and bearings subject to sacred words and timeless bonds. The one and only, Ferris Wheel.

Though abandoned, it had not crumbled. Though locked into unnatural stillness by creeping ivy, it was just as they had seen it in their visions. Just as they had always believed in.

La Grande Roue.

THE LIGHTHOUSE

This my castle stronghold, this my tower of light,
Across the ship-strewn waters, across the sea at night.

Through the stormy tempests,
and Nature's maddened cast,

This light shines out above them,
To safely let them pass.

VERSE

As far as the laws of mathematics refer to reality, they are not certain, and as far as they are certain, they do not refer to reality.

~Albert Einstein

Her hand accidentally smeared the ink across the college-ruled lines as her notebook flopped shut. The café was crowded, overly so, but just in time for the early lunch discounts. The elderly regular who had taken up residence next to her carefully nursed his handkerchief through a breakfast combo, picking through eggs and toast in a manner that seemed far too refined for someone who apparently dined in hell four days a week.

Stale coffee grounds and ketchup spills sketched out cracks of hazelnut nut and tomato into a bleached floor, a charmless Rorschach testament to the aesthetic genius of the masses. The lone waitress, not much more interested in the surrounding conversations than she was, had forgotten her hours ago for more promising tips all the while the matte glare of the faded green counter mirrored the soft din of a bustling Tuesday afternoon.

Feriha adjusted her headscarf self-consciously. It wasn't that anyone had commented on it but rather that she was still wary about being so obviously out of place, so clearly observed from all sides. Yet, she couldn't be the one observing back. Facing trial and judgement over two sugar packs and silence was asking a lot for a typical weekday, so she just continued to look down at the notebook. "Frankie" was scrawled on the cover in permanent marker.

Coming to college in the United States had always been her dream but the reality of it so far had been more complicated than Feriha had expected. Campus was lovely and the professors suitably distant. She'd made friends, signed up for clubs, and had been given an American name. Mostly out of convenience, she'd been led to believe and to avoid the frustration of having her actual name repeatedly misspelled and mispronounced. But now, sitting at the lunch counter, with her class notes clearly spread out as a sign that she belonged there, the name waved about like a white flag.

She had come for the equations, to find her ultimate comfort in numbers and signs, but first, she had to pass through the gates of lesser conformity. Her English was tested, despite the fact that she had been speaking it since kindergarten. Then, her mettle was tested, despite the fact that she had come alone, to a strange land, to dream of the same stars she could see from the rooftops of Istanbul.

Finally, her name had been reforged into the guise of something more fitting to the powers around her. In short, so that she might wear "Frankie" to distract everyone from noticing that she was also wearing başörtüsü. She despised the expressions of pity, concern, and sarcasm though. All Feriha wanted at that moment was to go back to her studies in the darkest corner of the library carrels she could find.

Astrophysics and literature might not strike the average passerby as worthy companions but to her, they were pure poetry. A combination of mysteries and meanings that could be woven together to create such awe, such wonder, as the world had never experienced before.

How comets could streak through the mystical words of Yunus Emre to create whirling galaxies befitting a jeweled dervish, or how the birth of planets coalesced into her nightly prayers, pouring all of her troubled soul out onto the ground and showing it to the moon. And the numbers, oh, the beautiful numbers that held it all. Arbitrary signs written with quick dashes that could mean anything or nothing but were somehow understood by everyone no matter where she was.

Sadly, one of her current literature books, a red-faced treatment of even older folklore in the guise of a science fiction publication following the fantastic adventures of one Captain Jonathan Nathanial Merchant, was so steeped in lurid prose that she couldn't help but think its cosmic nautical theme oppressive and its metaphorical lighthouses akin to a literary beating. It was a monologue of wishful thinking at best, merely unambitious at worst.

"For forty days and forty nights, I too had been swallowed up. Consumed wholly so by the passive motions of the beast that now swam through the stars, my lighthouse extinguished, and no path yet I could see. No path yet there was, no trailblazer's wake to follow in these endless waters."

However, lacking her own ambition, Feriha had long abandoned the task of raising the warm mug from the counter, opting instead to simply bring her lips down to it rather than risk the effort. Hunched over the chipped formica, she pulled a tube of purple lipstick from her pocket, idly twisting the container to smash the grape-colored cosmetic into the plastic cap.

She was irritable, her moods unpredictable and isolating. She hadn't been sleeping well for the better part of a week. If it wasn't a throbbing temple or stiff joint, it was a recurring nightmare that left her both disoriented and suffering from uncharacteristic night sweats.

From what she could recall, the strange dream involved her trying to swim the length of a giant lake filled with the ghostly corpses of whales floating just inches beneath the surface, smooth blue bodies suspended beneath the glassy water. She always had the impression that there was someone swimming beside her, but when she tried to look at them, they would immediately sink down into the murk, their face still blurred by the capriciousness of the unconscious mind.

Unable to rescue whoever it was, she would then find herself struggling to stay afloat and, towards the end of the ordeal, would end up fighting desperately for her life with the pillow and blankets. The dream never changed, she could never reach the far shore, and the sequence of events seemed more and more disjointed every time she woke from it. The last instance being only the night before, she was still feeling the effects of a long evening facing the fixed stares of the imaginary dead. This meant that between her professors and her dreams, it had been the week for oppressive nautical themes.

An exaggerated slurp got her attention long enough for her to look askance at the breakfast combo and handkerchief still perched on the far stool. She wrinkled her nose. He leered back. Abruptly, she swung her feet sideways, spinning the stool, and was out the door before the reflective plastic seat had finished a quarter turn. The book would make a fine enough tip for this adventure.

Frustration already threatening her fatigue, Feriha headed for the one place she knew her covered hair and long, flowing, sleeves wouldn't inspire a staring contest: the historical society building on the far end of campus. Across the quad with only six brief minutes in the company of humanity and she'd be safe again.

The grounds of Cornerstone State University were a sprawling mess of walkways and hills winding their way between the traffic of downtown Fairview and the relative serenity of the lakefront. Lake Hook, for its part, was nearly picture perfect even if the student-clogged arteries of the main thoroughfares were often choked with soda cans and in various states of warm weather construction.

Large boulders, glacially scattered throughout the grounds, were typically occupied by lone students taking their lunches in the sunnier months or by the occasional townie looking to escape the midday class changes. The local art museum, about half a block from the historical society, was the most conspicuous landmark along the way, its white-washed building a stark contrast to older brick and fieldstone structures that made up the rest of the freshman brochure.

It sat directly adjacent to the Catholic Student House, aptly nicknamed "the Catacomb," a towering Gothic building of cut stone more often used for weddings and marketing catalogs rather than any of the student organizations its outdoor boards were advertising.

The Student Union on her left, sporting a newly renovated cafeteria and arcade room, was by far the most popular destination in the main cluster of campus buildings and its position between the all-girls dorm on the hill and the obligatory row of fraternity houses up the street made it a perpetual three-ring circus long into the night. Feriha ignored it all and crossed the main courtyard, passed the Memorial Library (one of several libraries in the area), and turned toward the lower entrance to the museum.

She then paused to watch briefly as the sidewalks and expansive granite entrance stairs filled with people hurrying to their afternoon classes, wave upon strident wave of sneakers and cell phones. Within moments of the predictable crowd, a younger girl, not more than 13, appeared next to the largest mass cutting a swath through the quad, wearing a too-tight black t-shirt proclaiming that Jesus Saves.

Her cries of "Apocalypse at Hand!" and "Righteous Judgment!" garnered a number of wilting looks from her uninterested audience, but out of deference to her age, she remained carefully evaded.

Soon, unhappy with the apparent lack of the Holy Spirit's demanded presence in her work though, she quickly fixed on the layered headscarf and curve of black eyeliner that inevitably led to all of Frankie's social war stories.

"Miss?" The girl affected a subtle forward tilt before striking up a conversation. "Miss? May I talk to you for a moment?"

Feriha couldn't stop the heavy sigh from slipping out, but she managed to hide it under a forced cough before turning.

"Yeah. Sure. What's up, hey?" The smile was not genuine in the least.

"Have you accepted Jesus Christ, into your heart, as your personal Lord and Savior?"

The girl's halting, awkward, speech was the only sign that her nervous inexperience affected her. For a moment, Feriha felt almost sad. The likelihood that this small girl could account for even half of what was necessary for such a question killed the angry diatribe in her throat.

Squinting into the daylight, she tried quickly scanning the area for a likely parent or church leader, some measure of authority to hold accountable for this offense, but with only students between her and the street, she came up empty.

"Listen, I appreciate it but..."

The slick feel of a glossy pamphlet was pressed into her hand.

"God is...is...telling me that...he loves you and that he has a plan for you."

"I'll bet." Came the automatic reply.

"And that...that your greatest wish will come true if you are ready to ask him for it."

Feriha scowled. "Ok." she remarked flatly. "I wish to make contact with aliens."

"Aliens?"

"Yes. Aliens. People from another planet."

"Angels!" Her adversary squealed. "That's a great wish! I declare that an angel will visit you tonight!"

As the girl strode away, flush with newfound confidence, Feriha slowly shook her head and briefly wondered if this would be the young evangelist's proudest victory of the day. She moved with the poise of a standard-bearer. So, Feriha raised the pamphlet to rolled-eye level. 'Relief From Stress!' it screamed; pale orange letters sans serif splashed across the waxy paper. 'Let the Lord Guide You to Peace', deftly printed in a cursive-style font.

It was loud, bland, and unsettlingly uninspired for such eager declarations of immortal bliss. As the pamphlet fluttered to the ground, Feriha looked back to where the girl had been proselytizing moments before but saw no signs of her. She almost wished she was still there since she could almost think of something else to say now. But the girl was gone, denim skirt and subtle bouncing steps drowned in the baptismal rivers of born-again academia.

She turned back to the crusty museum door and slipped inside. It was the air of respectful silence she loved the most. Wandering the narrow halls of the Historical Society's museum wing was always intensely comforting, like crossing into a place of sacred contemplation when no one else was there. The soft hum of lights and fans, the distinctive scent of floor cleaner and age, always triggered some forgotten familiarity for her. She could recall numerous visits to museums like this one throughout her childhood, though the details of what she saw never seemed to accompany the memory.

Even so, the endless rooms of untouchable statues and artifacts had always held more appeal for her than many of the finer things in modern life. No amount of leisure and technology had ever meant as much to Feriha as the copper sistrum in Ankara, Foucault's Pendulum swinging listlessly in the corner, or the well-packaged meteorites; each in their own individually labeled white boxes.

Even the display mannequins of Neanderthal Man and the odd extinct bird or horse, posed almost comically in their glassy-eyed facsimiles of life, never failed to hold her attention each time she saw them. Neanderthal Man was always in need of a haircut, his brown flocking perpetually in disarray, and the Quagga looked like it could do with some patchwork and a few new hooves.

The forbidden specimen room was always top of the list though. Forbidden not because she lacked permission to enter, but forbidden in the way that visiting the raw, unwrapped, dead always felt to her. On shelves and tiered stands, in rows upon rows of browning glass jars, filled with sightless white eyes and matted hair, were all that had crept and crawled, flown and leapt, in days when man did not know that the world held more curiosities than would fill a single cabinet.

On any given day, she would pace the cases of reptiles and turtles or packed containers of beetles and worms or she might pause to lean in on the mice, gape at the fish, or ponder the two-headed oddities. On this particular day, she drew close to the stagnant vessels of birds and their like, arranged in long rows across numerous shelves and corner stands. Each jar held its captive wonder in a sickening monochromatic suspension, green or yellow with age and abuse.

Among the frayed feathers, Feriha could imagine bright orange and iridescent blue, hear high-note songs from beaks stuffed with cloth, and for a moment, could fill the room with the cacophony of angry creatures taken from their rightful places as dust in the ground.

She stared absently at the last jar in the second row, a drab sparrow marked with a crinkled paper tag, C28-724: Maine Passer domesticus No Date. It faced the back of its container, no more or less fascinating than any of the other forms except for its color, which over time had somehow managed to remain crisp and bright. Through the film that coated the glass, she could still make out rich browns and unfaded black, tiny specks of orange and yellow at the wing tips, and a slate-grey tail.

It was such a plain bird in life, now the crown of a poorly preserved aviary drowned for the sake of preserving its memory. The last bottled sparrow, so out of place from the rest, utterly captivated her now. All that followed was a sigh. Feriha, unusually tired for this early in the day, let her book bag slide to the carpet. As she left it there for the respite of the nearby bench, her senses were assailed with the smell of day-old coffee and mayonnaise.

No doubt the darker blue stain at her feet accounted for some of the trouble but the smell drifting from the covered trash can a few feet away wasn't likely innocent of the assault either. She scratched at her face, willing the impending headache into submission without success.

Closing her eyes, she tried to imagine a small team of workers, complete with long-handled brooms and Dickensian chimney sweep enthusiasm, scrubbing the black soot from the inside of her skull. Unfortunately, she quickly found that her cheerful band of conjured janitorial staff did little to ease the pain, and a complimentary regimen of continuous rubbing and twisting was equally as unsuccessful.

With another sigh, she simply gave up and retrieved the Tylenol bottle from her pocket. The headaches were becoming more frequent, sometimes one or two in a week, debilitating and intense, and contributed sporadically to her continued insomnia. She rattled the plastic bottle before swallowing two of the small tablets.

Her watch chirped, making unwelcome intrusions into the only actual solitude she enjoyed during the day. She glanced down, almost half past six, her forehead wrinkled in momentary confusion. She wasn't certain how the hour had gotten so late when she was sure that the early afternoon lunch specials should only just be finishing up, and now, the museum would be closing in less than thirty minutes.

Reluctantly, she reached over, wrapped her hands through the straps of her book bag, and gave it a heave, landing it squarely onto her shoulder. She wandered over to the jars again, one last look until tomorrow. There were the starlings and finches, all neatly arranged, and her sparrow, feet curled forward and cotton-packed eyes staring back at her, facing her through the glass.

She blinked. No, it faced the back of the jar. How else would she have known that its tail was grey? Feriha pinched the bridge of her nose, minding the pressure on her eyes. As the colored spots faded, and the world came into focus she stood motionless before the bird and jar.

A drab sparrow floating for eternity in the back of a struggling museum and nothing more. With nowhere else to be at that moment, she followed the late sun out of the main doors and back into the cooling air. The campus grounds were nearly deserted as students abandoned their hectic scrambling for the relaxed contentment of the downtown night scene. As Feriha began her slow walk back towards the far row of dormitory buildings, she caught the smell of rain hanging heavy in the air.

Always somewhat tainted by the smell of fresh tar and food vendors around the campus area, the earthy scent of the coming storm promised a long overdue cleansing of the littered grounds. Even a battered protest sign left lying on the curb, its wrinkled corners slowly collecting an assorted rainbow of trash in the street gutter, seemed ready to be washed away. Save the Whales. How fitting.

Blessedly, the promised storm didn't wait long. Intermittent tears of rain had already begun to fall by the time she reached Joseph Street Hall and, though it took some rough handling to pass the oblivious umbrellas, Feriha managed to slide into the main foyer just in time for the sky to retch and douse the unsuspecting and the unmoved.

Her shoes squeaked against the pale blue tile as she took the stairs two at a time, then through the rank hallways and past the rows of third-floor doors. Reaching the end, she shouldered the main door to her room, upsetting the delicate balance of stained photographs and magazine cuttings taped to the eggshell paint.

Her roommates, often easily lured into debates, could be found engaged in lengthy discussions in the main room, endlessly arguing over whether or not Emily Bronte was really a lesbian and what Diogenes' was actually looking for with his lantern. But in the end, it all still turned to celebrities, current events, and other colleges.

Having no choice but to listen to many of their late-night, lecture-fueled, rants, Feriha often found herself inadvertently drawn into the toe-to-toe confrontations between two predictably opposing sides. Last night's argument about Dr. MacCallister's "Rights of Man" lecture ended the communal philosophical consensus that all gods were the same god and had something to do with Schrödinger's cat and a bottle of water.

It was preceded by a heated discussion the day before about Dr. Kluger's presentation on gender politics in developing countries, a presentation that skirted terrifyingly close to eugenics and the nature of free will that also ended in numerous spontaneous disagreements. Several of her fellow students had then, of course, turned and looked at her before leaving.

The progression of these encounters had become predictable, and she couldn't help but feel the sting of a well-traveled road each time she offered up a quote or analytical thought to stifle rising tempers. Any attempt at instilling harmonious debate would be mistaken for arrogance and even then, uncertainty plagued her.

Feriha held no belief in intellectual superiority, but she felt weighed down by an undeserved sensation of repetition each time she engaged in these discussions. As though simply speaking was to trespass onto a toll road whose fee she had no intention of paying. In the end, she would just futilely criticize her own useless internal monologue for getting in her way again.

"Hey, Frankie!"

"Hey, Sara."

"What're you doing back so early?"

"Just here for my wardrobe consult."

"Very funny. Jack was looking for you earlier. I told him you weren't here because you joined a religious cult in Santa Barbara and were now going by the name of Moonfire Starpool."

Sara Psujek was ordinary in every way but one, her love of William Archibald Spooner. A notable brunette, with pale skin and Mediterranean features, Sara had arrived at Cornerstone as a transfer student two years ago. Now a linguistics major, she found endless amusement in aimless turns of phrase, New Age-sounding names, and making obvious social blunders.

"Moonfire Starpool, huh? Wasn't I just Butterfly Oakflower or something last week?"

"Keep giving me that look, and you'll be Jezebel Judas Mud." The wry grin curled over her face as she paced after Feriha into the empty room that served as the roommates' makeshift kitchen.

"Well, beats Frankie."

"Nah, it could be worse." Hands planted firmly on her hips, Sara took up her usual position in the empty doorway. "At least your name doesn't rhyme."

Sara's parents had briefly considered naming her Susan after a late, great-grandmother but after some consideration and no small amount of compassion on behalf of their unborn daughter, they decided to name her Sara in honor of her mother's favorite Jefferson Starship song. However, the still-favored Sue became her middle name and from then on, a secret source of adolescent embarrassment.

Rummaging through the remains of an open box of crackers, Feriha failed to notice as a slip of glossy paper drifted to the ground near her feet. Sara leaned in far enough to snatch it from the carpet, "What's this?" She turned it over in her hands. "Let the Lord guide you to peace, huh?"

Feriha looked up from the plastic Tupperware in her hands, "What? Let me see that." She tried unsuccessfully to twitch the pamphlet from the elder girl's hand, the bright letters and familiar candle-lit imagery giving her little doubt as to what it was.

"That's odd. I could've sworn I tossed that back in the quad."

Sara couldn't help but snort as she read the back of the booklet. The skin of her brow crinkled causing the characteristic downturn of the corners of her eyes whenever she laughed. With the loudest booming proclamation her alto voice could manage, tickled with mock authority, she read aloud.

"Did you know that true happiness will never be found in a store, a bottle, a pill, a syringe, or a bank account? Happiness is not for sale; it is free. Where can we find such a precious gift? Only in our Lord Jesus Christ!"

Feriha could almost hear her pronounce the exclamation point with an intentional upward lilt of her voice.

"Can you believe these people? Seriously."

Feriha held on to the crackers. A crumb fell onto her chin as her mind leapt into a memory, but it was not her memory. A small girl with blonde hair was beginning a Sunday morning dressed in her best pastels, hard-soled shoes, itchy tights, and a tiny, white hat with a spray of artificial yellow and purple flowers slowly becoming unglued from the brim. She was on her way to the Easter morning services of Blessed Savior Church with her mother and older brother, who, she thought at the time, were terribly lucky for not having to bear the burden of pink and white dresses that barely scraped the knees.

Blessed Savior was well known in her small southern hometown and was proud of its strictly literal interpretation of the modern Bible. At eight years old, she had had little understanding of the finer workings of faith, but she could clearly still smell the acrid steam of the percolated black coffee the elderly members of the Ladies Circle put out each morning. At promptly nine, the initial gathering of parishioners crowded the small lobby as the official greeters bustled about in search of new faces to usher in.

As conversations of daily lives and small-town gossip were lost on her, Feriha was drawn to a line of hand-made crosses set in repurposed flower pots filled with plaster. Obviously, the work of the previous year's Sunday School class, she looked solemnly down the line of potted icons and thought how strange it was that miniature gravestones should decorate a table filled with candy and cookies.

The church's bell began its summoning toll, inviting all those gathered to enter the main hall to begin the opening hymn; a dirge of a piece sung in slow, deep, tones. A hush spread throughout the faithful as lights were dimmed and organ music softened. Heads bowed and hands folded in prayer, the Benediction began but for the next hour or so, there would be no happiness in the miracle of resurrection. No happiness anywhere at all. There were no stars in the night sky painted overhead and for a flash in time, in another world, Feriha felt as if that little girl might have been her.

"Hey, Earth to Frankie."

In her mind, the visions continued. The girl scribbled a series of numbers on the back cover of her Genesis workbook. Then, she started to sketch a diagram that included the parts of an old computer keyboard connected with colorful wires to some kind of small television satellite dish. It was almost whimsical. Nonsense equations written in circles around maps of constellations that labeled a mishmash of machine parts she had been hiding beneath her bed. Every night, she would slide under the frame, next to the puffs of cat hair, and talk softly into the plug-in microphone for hours. Imagining someone, not too unlike her, was listening. A prayer that, in the end, she could only speak in secret.

"I said, Earth to Frankie!"

"Hmmm? Oh yeah, I know right? Seriously."

Sara chewed her lip thoughtfully over the fold of the pamphlet before discarding it into the trash.

"Hey, I'm meeting everyone at The Boathouse in a bit, why don't you come with? You could use a break."

Once again, the crackers failed her and Feriha realized that she had little chance of declining Sara's invitation to one of their favorite late-night restaurant haunts. The only thing left in the dorm room other than a few cans of soda was a bag of two-week-old marshmallows and, truthfully, they were losing their appeal in the face of an all-you-can-eat Tuesday night salad bar. The crackers were shortly abandoned for her boots and coat.

"You've convinced me. Let's go."

The rain sputtered onto the windshield in lazy drops as Sara steered the car through the glare of wrung-out streets. A low fog had begun to settle as the cool evening air drifted in from the lake and the lights of downtown Fairview were barely visible from Woogim's Coffeehouse on the corner of 1st Avenue to Carpe Musica a block away.

The night-time crowds had hardly diminished despite the downpour and the steady streams of boisterous groups filed past the windows as Feriha remained closed inside herself. Picking absently at a vinyl blemish in the door, she watched the passing scenes of blurred buildings and smudged pedestrians.

Splashes of neon lights created a painted canvas across the passenger side window, water slowly washing the colors away in rivulets over the glass. Her hand tentatively reached up, as though intent on smearing the world away in a single arc. For a moment, she smelled lilacs, a cloying scent drifting past her cheek and vanishing into the chill-soaked scent of water and pavement.

Sara turned left and pulled the car to an abrupt stop in a weedy parking lot near Fairview's east-side shopping malls. The Boathouse, while not actually located anywhere near water, sported a wide, open-faced, façade reminiscent of Scandinavian design and a dock-themed terrace extending out of the back.

Once inside, they quickly scampered through the grease-mist and the din of laughter, through the tapping of knives and forks, to their typical booth near the back windows. As usual, Kiran sat on the far left, across the table from Luke.

"Gentlemen," Sara announced, collapsing onto the edge of the booth.

"Hey hey." They both responded in kind.

Feriha smiled and waved, as was her typical greeting, before sitting down opposite Sara and next to Kiran.

"What've you two been up to?" Luke started off.

"Frankie got caught by the Jesus Freaks again."

"Seriously?"

Feriha shrugged. "Not like it's a surprise." She replied. "But it sucks that they're using little kids to do it now."

Kiran leaned back. "What do you mean?"

"It was this girl, maybe ten or eleven. She just seemed, I don't know, so excited about it all. You can't even get that mad about it. She doesn't know any better. No clue what kind of life she might have had if things had gone differently."

"Yeah but," Luke interrupted. "Isn't that true of everybody? I mean, I could just have easily ended up in some office job getting my kicks on the internet rather than here."

Feriha sighed, even though no one heard it. "True. It just makes me a little sad, I guess. So much out there. So much we don't know. I could imagine all kinds of different lives she might have had that don't involve throwing Bible verses at every woman she sees with a headscarf."

Kiran nodded. "Exactly. I mean, I always imagined that I'd start a band and get famous. Thrash my way straight to the top! But no! I have to go pre-med first. Parents orders."

Luke laughed. "Right. The next Punjabi metalhead."

"Bro, I'll have you know that..."

But Feriha already couldn't hear them over the roar of a football chant erupting from the far side of the dining hall. It wouldn't have mattered that her words were carried off by incoherent hoots anyway though. Her answer was for herself alone.

"I've always dreamed of discovering life on other planets. Of being the person on the other end of the scanner when we hear those first words of contact. I used to play it out in my mind all the time. Don't think I'm the only one either..."

She had another dream that night. This time she stood next to a young Black girl as she leaned over the balcony of her high-rise apartment building. Her braids dangled over the railing as she pushed further than was safe. Before Feriha could say anything, the girl spoke.

"Look at that." She breathed excitedly. "Can't you see it?"

Far below, the city stretched on for miles until it reached a harbor. But from this distance, it all looked like a series of random geometric shapes and patterns in grey, brown, and blue.

"See what?" She asked.

"The sparrows." The girl answered. "Watch how they move, how they calculate distance, time, and speed in an instant to get any point on any building. Perfect landing, every time. They don't even know they're doing it; that's the best part. It's just how they see the world. It's how they see the angles or the corner turns."

Feriha watched what the other girl watched and saw only flocks of birds murmurating through the street grids. "I don't see it," she said. "They're just birds."

The girl smiled back at her. "Right. And what any kid in the projects would give to fly just like them." Feriha was then appraised with a stern look. "You must be Frankie. I'm Basti."

"Am I dreaming?"

"We're all dreaming, that's kind of the whole thing. Ali said you were a little thick."

"Who.... who?"

"You met my friend, Ali. Earlier today."

"Wait, wait, the girl with the Jesus shirt?!"

"What? Girl, no! After you saw my sparrow."

Feriha was terribly confused. Reality was dissolving and her memories started to become jumbled. "A...a church. At Easter? She had this pink dress with a white hat. Potted.... crosses in pots?"

Basti broke up laughing. "Aw, lordy. Yeah, that's Ali. She hated that hat. So much she gets stuck back in that moment sometimes. What an intro right? But it's where it all started. It's where she first came up with the design for the radio."

"Ok." Feriha stepped back from the edge, shaking her head. "Now I know I'm losing it. This isn't real. None of this is real. I'm just hallucinating after a night of no sleep while my roommates argue about truth and morality or something."

Basti uncrossed her arms and pursed her lips with concern. "The radio, Frankie. That's why you're here. Well, ok, technically it's a multisensory electromagnetic converter but it doesn't matter, it works! Sure, we both had our junk projects when we were kids. Pretending we could talk to outer space.

But once we got together on that campus, we figured it out! SPARROW, we called it, of course. It was Ali's equation about the wave. Like a flight path. Short undulations, a series of quick beats, and then a short free-fall. Remember that, ok? No swoop, no pump. Just remember the pattern. Long wavelength, low frequency; that's what everybody does. But then the beats and the fall all the way down."

"Basti, what am I supposed to do with that? I'm not an engineer, I'm just..."

"The one who always dreamed you'd be on the other end of the radio."

Feriha had no response.

"Find SPARROW. It's all yours now. Pick up where we left off."

"Wait, where are you? I don't understand, why can't you show me yourselves?"

"Nah." Basti shrugged with a wry grin. "We just memories now. Ali and Basti, together forever."

Feriha woke suddenly and with a deathly cold shiver.

Her dorm room was quiet. Or, as quiet as dorm rooms ever got at Cornerstone. The walls might as well have been cardboard for all the sound they kept out but, for once, she couldn't be bothered to even notice. She wrapped her headscarf quickly and probably a little sloppily but after throwing on the rest of her clothes, the entire image came together rather well despite it.

It was late, but clearly not too late, because although the sky was fighting back against the college's overly large street lights, there were still occasional students trodding the worn sidewalks. Feriha ignored them all as she frantically searched for the lower museum door. It was more of a feeling than an actual memory, but she just knew she had to find that last bottled sparrow one more time.

Blessed Allah, the door was open, and she thanked every saint she could think of for the janitor's habitual lateness in finishing his closing duties. Nonetheless, she stepped through as quietly as she could. From there it was the halls of grand exhibits, past the rows of interactive kiosks, and the finally down the stairs to the older collections.

Immediately, she homed in on her sparrow; the same ragged little bird floating in macabre suspension behind a jar at least a hundred years old. But it was actually the tag that she wanted to see closer. Some vague part of her mind seemed to be holding on to a not-quite-memory of a stamp on the corner of the curled paper. Something that had to be relevant, she was sure of it. And then, there it was.

C28-724: Maine Passer domesticus

And barely visible on the edge of the tag: Donated by Miss Laila "Ali" Dorfeld. Feriha's jaw dropped. Cornerstone had a building named after her, Dorfeld Hall. It had once been a dorm back when the college was founded but now served as the science center. Ali Dorfeld was famous, in fact. As was her colleague, Basti Dayo Naserian; the founder of the very astrophysics lab she had spent countless hours in, daydreaming and absent-mindedly solving for x.

"Funny how these things start, isn't it?" The voice behind her startled Feriha so badly she momentarily froze in place, unable to turn around or even scream. Finally, though, but with great effort, she slowly turned around.

An old woman, hunched over a cracked cane, looked back at her. Dressed oddly, in a pink and white shift that barely fit her, white tights with colorful felt stripes on the ankles, and a hat. A white straw hat with fake flowers on the brim, slowly becoming unglued. Her eyes, wrinkled to the point of almost completely obscuring the pinpoints of light behind the black void of her pupils, squinted as she looked Feriha over. Her voice, however, was strong.

"Before you ask, yes, you're dreaming. So, don't even bother. Wait, no, I'll do you one better. You're psychic. That's what this is."

Feriha choked. "Psychic? I'm psychic now? I think maybe you mean I'm just going crazy. You have no idea what today has been like, I..."

The woman raised her hand. "I know exactly what it's been like. Same as for me. Same as for Basti. Not that we knew any of that until we had the great universal fortune of getting assigned to the same dorm room. Though it wasn't fortune really, so I shouldn't say that. Just an inevitable murmuration."

"You…you're Ali Dorfeld, aren't you? But you're dead. You have to be. You'd be, like, a hundred and fifty or something."

"Basti would say memories. I say that once you solve an equation, it stays solved. At least, in some respects. I found the constant to my variables, got to the answer I was going to get. Now, it's where you'll have the chance to start. Keep going. Find your answer, pass it on. Psychic-like." She laughed.

"There are no such things as psychics." Feriha held her ground but could feel the fear shaking the base of her skull. She was becoming convinced that she was actually haunted and that these were the ghosts of museum row. "Just, maybe, mutations or something."

"Psychic isn't a mutation, it's a phenomenon."

"Ok, semantics."

The old woman sighed and swept right in with a professorial tone. "What is psychic but a leap in perception beyond what is considered normal? A biological characteristic based on the electrical conductivity and reactivity of the brain isn't out of the question.

This particular trait is not uncommon among women as it turns out, though it seems that all genders are capable of expressing the trait under the right circumstances. My dear, this is not some random mutation, but a genetic sequence recessively passed down among humankind for many generations now.

It stands to reason that there would come a time where a predictable leap in evolutionary combinations would endow particular humans with the ability to perceive the fourth spatial dimension. Thus, psychic."

Feriha wasn't convinced, and by Ali's expression, it showed.

"I see. You want the science. But I'm afraid you'll need more than math to get out of this conundrum. Maybe a story. Think of it like this. Imagine a playing card face-down on a table. All those in attendance now perceive this three-dimensional object in a three-dimensional perspective."

"But isn't the card two-dimensional?"

"No, three dimensional, simply a very thin three dimensions." She continued, "The psychic, however, actually perceives the cards four dimensionally and by that, she is able to turn the mirror image of that space backward around itself and see the opposite side of the card before returning her normal perception to that of the back of the card. For some, this would almost be as though the psychic had taken a piece of space and time and turned it around so that she could view it from the other side. This is why it can seem that the perception of four dimensions is a form of time travel, jumping into the future to glimpse an imminent event before returning to predict it, when in fact, it is a rather simple matter of spatial relations."

Feriha tried her best. "So, you're saying that because the face-down image of the card already exists at various moments in time and space, viewing it is a matter of vantage point?"

"Close enough. At least, that's close to what Basti understood. Waysmiths. That was the word she like better."

"You mean to tell me that there are people out there who can somehow tether themselves to a single point in time and space, and then flip it or themselves around, moving…tesseracting their view into impossible…" she paused, at a loss. "Sorry, but what kind of fairy tale ridiculousness is this? What the hell are you and why are you talking to me?"

"Because — Feriha — as you may have already noticed, that is precisely what you are doing right now. I'm not a ghost. What you saw in that church and on that balcony weren't hallucinations. They were, they are, points set within a particular time and in a specific space we designated and anchored. Basti on the balcony of her mother's apartment. Me, at church. Me, here now with one of Basti's sparrows. Our little trail of breadcrumbs through the forest, if you will. But you have likely also noticed that these places were not devoid of matter. These weren't visions, not like a 'vision' when people typically say that word anyway. This, Feriha, this is where we ended, and you must begin."

"I just...I just don't understand what you want from me."

"Remember the patterns and think. To simply stop in one point in space and time and turn into another without any form of conscious control would result in an almost certain catastrophic explosion as the three-dimensional matter of your body came into contact with the motion of your three-dimensional world moving through four-dimensional space. By that token, only one who can perceive all angles of motion is capable of course-correcting in time to avoid collisions, thus... finding the Way. And the Way is the only chance you'll ever have of finally achieving your dream. The dream of knowing what's really out there."

"Uh-huh. And Oz is over the rainbow."

"No, it's in the basement."

Museum basements were the forbidden dungeons of legend. Filled with treasures and oddities of all kinds. Boxes, some labeled, some worn to nothing but grasscloth threads, were stacked in haphazard rows on a stone floor that looked as though it had flooded at least twice. Feriha navigated her way through towers of old pots, terrified she'd catch the corner of some flaked sherd and bring the whole thing crashing down around herself.

But her sense of floating, flowing along with the tides almost, kept her moving. Each glass-mounted manuscript she passed felt like another island in the storm and suddenly the dashing extravagance of old Captain Jonathan Nathanial Merchant didn't seem so bad anymore. The writing was still terrible, on both counts.

On the far side of the cellar though, she spotted what the mirage of Ali Dorfeld had told her she would find. A seam in the cinderblocks, obscuring a rotten wooden door that had once led to the original boiler room. After the museum had modernized in the 1990s however, nothing inside of it had been of any use, so the docents had simply closed it up and walked away — ironically preserving what was barely hidden. Had they taken but a single moment to explore the shadows beyond, they might have found what was truly wondrous about the dank, moldy, places of Cornerstone.

Feriha slipped inside, smearing dirt across her chest as she forced a small opening at the edge of the soggy wood. Dim light from a culvert window cast everything around her into faint blue lines scribbled together by the fractals of spiderwebs thickened with dust. Behind the iron columns of the steam boilers, relics of another era themselves, was a table. It looks like it had been made piecemeal out of scraps; planks taken from shipping crates and supports stolen from pallets.

It had then been painted green to blend in with the surrounding tool cabinets. But what sat at its center was nothing short of a marvel. Wires tumbled in every direction, connected by twisting tape to every conceivable input and output. Parts of various transmitters were stacked together underneath a Futaba radio control box, which itself had then been hooked up to myriad disassembled parts of a Crystal radio and an Altec 690A transistor telephone. It was like staring at the abandoned leftovers of a time capsule that hadn't made it out of the early 1970s.

A strange sense of sadness washed over Feriha. For a moment, she thought she could see two indistinct figures of a pair of young women, bustling around a homemade switchboard covered in paper notes indicating the orbital equations of various satellites.

They had been so deeply inspired by watching the first moon landing that their linked passions for discovery burned hotter than any coal fire. They argued over rates of circumpolar decay and giggled with joy as Basti unveiled a bag crammed with purloined equipment, including an echo canceller, a Trifield EMF meter, and the box of a broken microwave. Feriha looked around herself in awe.

This was a lab. This was Ali and Basti's lab. The place where they had met, for years while in college together, building their own communications device to contact outer space. The machine: SPARROW. The one they had built with dreams of being the first humans on Earth to contact alien life. If only they could overcome the Fermi Paradox.

As any first-year astrophysics student learned, the Fermi Paradox referred to the aggravating discrepancy between the lack of conclusive evidence of advanced extraterrestrial life and the apparently high likelihood of its existence. Meaning, in short, that due to the vastness of the universe, other worlds with other intelligent life forms essentially must exist by statistical probability alone.

Any yet, none had ever become conclusively known in all of human history. To her memory, most scientists chalked up the problem to the incredible distances between stars and their planets. Or to the simple fact that any other suitably advanced civilization just might not be listening in on radio waves within the spectrum of human hearing.

It was with a jolt of insight then that Feriha suddenly realized what Ali and Basti had been trying to tell her the entire time. That they had solved the Fermi Paradox. It wasn't space, it was time. The true dilemma of contacting other worlds wasn't just limited by the human imagination, it was a problem of perception. A problem, she murmured to herself, of vantage point.

With a rush, she cleared off as much of the debris covering the table as she could, sifting through papers and making piles she would pour over later. She brushed off the machine and began to study the schematics laid out next to it, feeling excitement rising in her chest in a way she could barely remember it. It was all here. Everything she needed to…

…there was a long slip of paper laid out near her left hand. The end of it still stuck inside the printer mouth it had slid out from. It looked like a thin segment of receipt paper, with a smudge of yellow ink staining the bottom half. Next to the decaying slip, a pocket notebook lay open to a mostly empty page. In a woman's loopy penmanship, the two hastily jotted diagonal lines read:

Steven was right.

"I am, somehow, less interested in the weight and convolutions of Einstein's brain than in the near certainty that people of equal talent have lived and died in cotton fields and sweatshops."

Where is Frankie? Someone had then written. How do we find her?

This caused Feriha to stare down at the curled-up printout with even more trepidation. But she had to know. Where had Ali and Basti ended, and why? Where was she about to begin?

Where is Frankie? They had written and then left.

With careful fingers, she turned the paper over, trying desperately not to tear it. She could barely make out the old block letters and green ink that had been spit out by the 1971 dot matrix printer but in lying face down, the message had somehow been saved from fading completely. She tilted her head and mouthed the words. Then, she gasped and fell to her knees, the paper breaking away from the machine and wrapping around her arms like a wide ribbon.

WE HEARD YOU, FRANKIE. WE KNOW WHO YOU ARE. YOU ARE NOT READY. WE ARE NOT COMING.

Ammonite and Trilobite went out to the Tethys Sea,
Veering off a simpler age but shelled as sterns could be.
They trundled on most unaware, until the tide turned cold.
Whereas a spiral said to a spine, "Look up, my friend, behold!"

A mountain formed right from the waves, and the water drained away.
They drifted then on tides of air, through clouds and wind and clay.
It was Ammonite who then leapt aloft, "Off with us now, let's go!"
"The sea is done, we're up to the sun, and the salt has turned to snow!"

But the Trilobite went sour at this, for he had no clout nor speed,
"I cannot float, and I do not swim, how might I proceed?"
"On my back, bend to my curve!" the Ammonite exclaimed.
"Pin your pleura to my conch, new adventures are unclaimed!"

"That can't be true," Trilobite grumped, but still did as he was told.
Though on that husk, a funny thing, his calcite eyes saw gold.
Such unlikely friends, these mismatched two, mixed up against the odds.
An epoch late, men then observed, Olenus rode cephalopods.

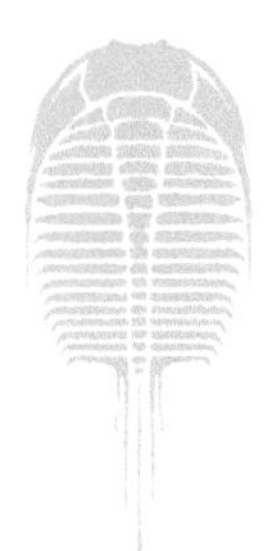

Down they trudged, through mud and rain, slow as slow could be.
Eons passed but they paid no mind, to fern then shrub then tree.
"Where are we going?" Trilobite asked, weary from cleavish cuts.
"To the river, my friend!" Ammonite said, after we stop by the huts.

"No one will see the reeds that I pick, and from there I'll make us a boat!"
"A beautiful vessel, both long and soft, with tufts of a pashmina goat!"
"From there," the Ammonite mused, "we'll set off to Laurentia's coast."
"My cousins are there, with their New World flair, ready to play as our host."

"But where is our convoy, and the belemnite squids?" The Trilobite fussed with grief.
"Asleep in the stone without help of bone." As Ammonite sewed up a sheaf.
"That's why it's us and blessed that way, don't you see we were meant to last."
"Now off to a future with new life and new tales, while they'll be stuck in the past."

So off they both went, in a boat made of stalks the Ammonite plucked from the shore.
Taking their turns through white-water churns, across countryside they now could explore.
They saw towering faces carved right into rock and a temple with wheels made of birch.
But it rolled down a hill and smashed on a cliff, so that was the end of that church.

Next there was a giant, drawing lines in the sky, using stars to make pictures of beasts.
These monsters on canvas then smeared out the light and mocked his facile beliefs.
When he tried once again to trace them as maps, they just hid below the horizon.
So, the giant traded his paints for a jar, whose end he could then press his eyes in.

At last, they passed a unicorn's woods, where a dodo bird shrieked out a curse.
"Not the likes of me, will anyone see, it has come down to the worst."
"It's all bureaucrats, with their ships full of rats, and now I must fly away."
But he spread his short wings that could not take flight, thus knowing he'd have to stay.

From there a great valley, painted in red, rose up on all sides but one.
It narrowed and merged into a frightening surge, up and over they spun.
The water rushed past, but they clung on as fast, to shields of chitin and pearl.
Yet they could not be saved, sad as it was, from falling out into the whirl.

When there they looked out from the Ammonite's spout, a cave stretched far overhead.
It was stale and hot, with sharp crystal spots, and the Trilobite felt nothing but dread.
"There!" Said his friend, with an Ammonite's zeal, "It's filled with glitter pink salt!"
"Here's where it's gone, down here is our sea, simply by dint of a fault!"

The ground then did shake with a rattling roar, an earthquake climbed up from the depths.
The heat grew so thick that the stone became quick, and it flowed out onto the steppes.
The little reed boat bobbled on steam, pushing up on a basaltic landslide.
Ammonite and Trilobite could paddle no more and simply held on horrified.

They twirled and swirled until it all came to rest on a small sandy cove with a ridge.
The water was cool in the bustling pools, with news brought only by midge.
With sighs of relief, they dug into loam and cherished hyperborean rime.
Side by side they remained, until earth became stone, chatting amiably to pass the time.

They talked of kelp and their favorite grits, snug in their beds of lime.
The new seas moved in, and the old seas moved out, but they missed the freedom of brine.

They longed to swim off into an unexplored gorge, and wallow in the lull of the deep.
Instead, they stayed put and mumbled goodnight as they strayed off into a wistful sleep.

Then suddenly a hammer fell, near to cleaving them both in twain.
But a gentler hand brushed off the dust, revealing the Spiti plain.
And so, Ammonite and Trilobite went back out in the Tethys Sea,
In a little tote made of cotton rope, at a height of forty-one twenty-three.

This was the end! They'd be crushed into gravel! Went Trilobite's diatribe.
But the man with the bag had engravers hands along with a pneumatic scribe.
He cleaned them up and set them out, mumbling nothing but flattery.
Put under a dome so they could see their new home, the two friends saw a gallery!

They saw the old temple with its broken-up cart, now a wagon with spokes in its wheels.
It sat next to a ship also encased, with a white whale devouring its keels.
By that sat the dodo bird, beak in a scowl, also permanently on display.
"This is an insult! It was never just so!" He shouted at the unmoving fray.

"They cut down my trees and shot with their guns, it was not just some cachalot!"
Dodo huffed, tattered feathers all fluffed, "You'd think they'd killed a dreadnaught!"
Ammonite turned to his friend with concern, "I think he has lost his mind."
"Oh, I have!" Said the bird, their spurious third, "It's nothing but cotton and twine!"

And the giant was there with his jar full of lights, but the glass was a telescope.
Angled up at the ceiling, so dizzying high, that the stars caused a zoetrope.
Portraits of Ptolemy and Galileo too, hung in so many circles of men,
That Ammonite and Trilobite feared it aloud; what would become of them?

The people came in and the people went out, a sea of bright faces in wonder.
At two little shapes, a spiral and spine, whose camaraderie seemed such a blunder.
But they had been friends going on millions of years, eternity just out of focus.
It all had passed in less than a blink and five extinctions they'd barely noticed.

You can still see them today, if you pull out a drawer, in a museum poised on the highland.
Curios from a menagerie with tiny fish next to footprints in Thailand.
They're far down the hall in the darkest dank space, with every forgotten text.
And if you're quiet while there, you might hear them declare, "Where are we off to next?"

HUSH BY ADAM WASSIL

Asleep
A dream, a bite
To eat, we slip between
The dark and breathe in deep your sound
Asleep.

THE DREAM EATER BY ADAM WASSIL

It's a lucky thing that teddy bears can't roll their eyes. If they could, the knight Light would have rolled his eyes so hard that they just might've fallen from his big, fuzzy head and rolled themselves away altogether.

Why do they always try to hide, he slumped.

The teddy squashed a curtain's ruffles flat to the wall, snorted, and gave the fabric a bit of a toss.

The hiding itself didn't give the little knight any trouble, really. It was annoying, is all it was. This was Light's home, and he had been playing hide and seek here with his girl, Fiona, since before she was even walking. They'd played tag, they'd gone on adventures, they still buried treasure together from time to time – he'd grown up sussing out and sharing secrets with this house. How could these silly fey whats-its find their way here and hope to outwit him on the board he'd choose to play on every time?

It isn't just annoying, Light thought, it's kind of insulting, isn't it?

I'm insulted.

He would have a big problem on his small hands if the creeping fairy-thing woke either Fiona or her mother while he was out on his own, though. According to the human rules, teddies aren't supposed to be on patrol, after all, even if it is their duty to keep their houses safe from all the other-side-stuff while the rest of the world is asleep. It certainly didn't help that the house was as old and lived-in as it was; there were more than a few noisy traps the bear just had to hope the night fairy missed.

He knew them as well as he knew his own stitching, of course, but the intruder wouldn't know anything about the fourth and fifth steps or how they were the two loudest pieces of wood nature had ever produced. It wouldn't know that the ceiling fan's pulls were tiny bells from a holiday sweater that had been retired and that nothing had any business being that jangly, honestly, or that –

A tiny tink drew Light's black, beaded eyes upward, and he slumped again.

Or that Fiona crowds any flat surface she can find with figurines, he thought.

Another tinkle, the scuff of a felted base, and, sure enough, the quiet *rr-rr-rup!* of porcelain sliding into free-fall.

Four legs and a mane the color of old bones dove to meet an unwilling patch of floorboards.

"Not tonight, Horsey," Light grunted as he sprang forward.

The bear leapt and snatched the fragile pony, curling his fluffy body around it as it fell. He boffed about before coming to rest in the corner. The ball of Light waited there for several *tick-tick-ticks* of the wall clock, listening. There was another jingling sound, one that Light didn't quite recognize at first, but then a sibilant whisper slithered out from the shadows of the shelf, and the teddy realized it had been a laugh.

The sneaking fairy was laughing at him.

"A worthy save, you stuffy-brave," it hissed, "but let's see how well you're really made!"

Oh, no, Light thought as he looked up to his enemy. There was a gaunt little thing peering down at him, old-man-ish and naked behind a waterfall of beard flowing out from its sunken face.

Naked except for a slouching, red cone of a hat atop its head, the teddy noticed.

It was an alp, a dream eater, and it looked like they hadn't eaten in some time. A round and warted nose burst out from above the white spray of its beard, and its jaws were locked into a maniac grin, exultant, displaying far too many teeth for a head so small. It was straining against another porcelain statuette, laughing its tinkling laugh.

"How 'bout two," the hat-wearing elfling buzzed as they perched a pair of statuettes just at the shelf's edge, "here on the brink. Can you catch them both, you think?"

Light stood for a moment, his head tipped to one side as irritation bloomed behind his black eyes like poison in a well. "Are you rhyming on purpose?" he asked.

"I'm sorry? Come again?" The alp craned their stringy neck forward, a hand cupped cartoonishly to one ear as if it were struggling to hear. "I don't think I caught that, friend."

"Cut it out," the teddy said flatly, a touch of menace creeping into his otherwise soft voice. "Please. You need to leave here, but if you don't -"

"What's this? A plea? An attempt at parlay?" The elf's shaggy eyebrows lifted, "If indeed it is so, it's a shameful display for it sounds less like speech, alack and alas, and more like the braying of a dimwitted ass." They grinned again, giving Light a good look at every single one of their too-many teeth.

The bear let Horsey clatter to the floor as he stood rigid, his paws balled into fists.

"Oh, I'll very much -" the laughing fey began, ready to shove, before sputtering out a startled, "Wah!" and falling to their bony rump. Where their head was a moment before, a knitting needle jutted from the drywall, vibrating like a tuning fork. The alp's victorious grin had frozen into a shocked little "O" as they looked from the thrumming needle down to the bear.

"I *hate* rhymes," Light spat, hefting a second needle to his shoulder. That wasn't exactly true, though – he didn't hate rhymes so much as he was bad at rhyming, and the occasional fairy's preference to speak only in them reminded him of how poor his rhyming was.

"...You what?" the fairy blinked, seeming genuinely confused.

"Nevermind," Light grumbled before hurling the second needle at the fairy, javelin-style.

The alp didn't wait for the spike, though. The fey's red hat lit up with the glow and hum of fairy magics as their scrawny little body zipped out into the air above the bear's head. They snagged the needle mid-flight with astonishing speed and, angling its point straight down, launched themselves like a meteorite at an unready Light.

Ready or not, the bear dove into another roll, and the fairy's savage plunge missed him by the scruff of his tail at most. When the little knight regained his feet, he had produced a short, wooden sword. The fairy tried to pull the now-stuck needle from the floor by hand, but it ended up just grunting and tugging to no avail. It was proper stuck. Muttering, the elf made a few magical passes of their hands, and the knitting needle pulled itself from the floor.

It swished through the air around the alp with a fencer's flourish before coming to rest above their shoulder, floating on its own and aimed with intention at the battle-ready bear.

"Be careful, bear, how hard you play – you could hurt someone someday," the alp said darkly, their eyes glittering with the arcane glow curling up from their flexed and clawed hands.

"If you think this is a game, fairy," Light entreated, "I suggest you stop playing right now."

"It's still just honking like a goose," the alp said with a resigned sigh, lifting their hands in a small shrug. The needle bobbed with the rolling of their shoulders. "If we can't discuss, then... have at you!"

The alp exploded into motion. Their fingers flicked and wriggled like sharp little worms half-burrowed into their palms. They shimmered with that weird fairy light as the dream-eating thing raked them through the air like a conductor leading a silent symphony of one. The tumbling needle danced to whatever mystic tune the alp whispered to it, flying and swinging and stabbing in time with the fairy's herky-jerk hand movements.

Maybe it'll keep its mouth shut when it's fencing, Light hoped, fending off the fairy's blows. After a few parries, he added, *At least I understand it's skulking now, though. It isn't exactly an artist with a sword.*

Unfortunately for the alp, though, Light was exactly that.

The rhythmic *pok-pak-pok-ing* of the needle against Light's wooden sword wouldn't be enough to bother anyone, he didn't think, and the bear had taken a full enough measure of the alp during those first few moments. In no time at all, the elf was sweating.

It's getting worn out fast, Light thought.

Good.

"I think we're about done here, elfling," the fuzzy knight said, stepping from his defensive, two-handed posture into a duelist's stance, his sword-hand leading, his blade raised.

"The bear still squawks as though it speaks," the alp panted, frustration breaking through its lack of breath. "But I hear no meaning within its beak."

The bear lunged at the alp with such a ferocious chop that the night elf had no choice but to use their hands as well as their magics to keep the knight from hacking into it. The squeaking alp's knees buckled as the teddy drove it down further, chopping into the smooth, metal spike with swing after heavy swing. Light brought his sword up for the strike that would certainly be the kneeling alp's last, and they both knew it.

But when the sword fell, the only thing it landed on was an unlucky hallway floorboard. The alp twisted like an adder and struck out at Light's sword hand. The little fairy clamped onto the bear's soft wrist, and the two began to tussle and roll and bop one another like schoolyard ruffians until someone got a leg in the mix and shoved. The alp and the bear tumbled apart.

Springing to their feet, the alp thrust not one, but two weapons toward the roof with a triumphant hoot. In one hand, their own borrowed weapon of choice, the knitting needle, and in the other, they held the teddy's wooden blade.

"Oh-ho-ho! Oo-hoo-hoo! We each had one, but now I've two! Lookie-here, my lookie-loo, and tell me now, what say you?"

"Checkmate," the teddy said, dusting himself off as he stood. The fey thing gave the bear a blank look before Light added, "Like I said, we're done here, elf. I've got your-"

The alp stomped their foot several times, interrupting the bear, before pointing Light's own sword at him and all-but-shouting, "Listen here, you silly thug, you seem to think I'm being smug when I tell thee, sir – and I tell thee true – I cannot grasp the words you use!"

Light's shoulders slumped. The little bear often felt like sighing – he couldn't actually sigh after all, considering – but he couldn't remember a time he felt any more like he should be able to.

After a few moments of thought, he looked up, then back at the alp.

"I maybe lost the tit-for-tat, but now I've got your magic hat," he said with a shrug, holding up the alp's red hat. The bear took a brief peek inside the hat with a discerning eye before he set it atop his head and gave it a good snugging on over his ears.

The alp couldn't do anything but stare, slack-jawed, as both of their new trophies fell to the floor. Their sinewy fingers jumped to their bald and now-bare scalp, *plap-plapping* over their skull with clammy little palms.

"My... my hat," they started. Their face snapped from an uncomprehending disbelief to an animal fury in an instant. "You dare?!" the darkling roared, "How dare you?! How-"

"Hush," the bear said, making a few bland passes with his paw. The familiar glow of fairy magic danced along the wispy tips of his fur and within the felt of the hat, and the alp's jaws snapped shut.

"You..." the alp ground out through gritted teeth, "you know how to ply the magic of... my kind?"

"Well, yeah," Light offered blandly, stepping forward to retrieve his sword. After sparing it a glance, it began to melt in his grip, bleeding as it did into a trail of tumbling leaves. The leaves twisted in a lazy whirl before they crumbled to dust, and then the dust itself dissolved like a curl of smoke. "My sword was a gift from the fairy world, and it was enchanted by the Wardens of the Nightmare Wood." Light rested his heavy gaze upon the alp. "You aren't the first fairy I've met."

The now-powerless alp tried their best to run away from this stoic sentry who seemed no less competent with sorceries than he did with swordsmanship. They tried their best, but failed in this, too. As they sprang into the air, they found theirself caught fast – or caught slow, rather – in some unseen zone of weightlessness.

Instead of bounding down the hall, the outsider merely floated like a bubble on its way up to the top of a honey jug. In the midst of their painfully sluggish arc, Light fell in step beside them.

"Please," the elf started, but the teddy quieted them with another pass of one glittering paw.

"What are we going to do with you?" the teddy knight asked more to himself than the alp. He stooped again, picking the knitting needle up. We wouldn't want Fiona stepping on it in the morning, after all. Mornings could be a hectic thing in the Guthrie household. He'd need to get the other needle from the drywall, though – hectic or not, they'd likely notice that.

"Please," the alp sputtered out again through their magically locked jaws, "let me go, let me leave, and I swear to you, I'll leave you be."

"Hmm," Light considered the needle at length. "If I just do away with you proper, that won't be a problem, I think."

The night fairy started whimpering then, and doing their best to swim out of the magical hold the teddy had over them. If Light were any more cruel, he might've laughed at the spectacle. He didn't, though. He merely tipped his head in thought.

It must have been a menacing tilt, though, for the alp burst out, "I'll do anything you say! Everything!" they cried, "I'll do everything you say, just don't kill me! I swear, I-"

"Deal."

"I promise, I s-what?" The alp froze, now stuck in a balletic, zero-gravity turn very much out of their control.

"You have a deal, I said," Light repeated, and all at once, the magic was dismissed, and the small night fairy hit the floor with a heavier whump than Light expected. He only felt a little bad about it. "In exchange for your life, you will do anything – and everything – that I say. And I say that you will continue to do 'anything and everything that I say' until I release you from your bondage. Well-struck, Elf."

A bargain. The alp sat in a crabby sprawl, staring up at the bear that just stuck them within the confines of a bargain. The teddy bent over it, took the hat from his own fuzzy noggin, and plopped it back onto his new fairy-side friend's bald head. Light gave it a smart straightening up, then put his paws beneath the little fairy's arms and hoisted them to their feet.

"There you are," he said, giving the alp a few pats. "Now you can go."

The alp's face was a roiling thing at that moment, a pot so hot that it was ready to boil its rage and shame all over onto the floor, but as they opened their mouth to give vent to any of the warring emotions rumbling about beneath that magic red hat, the bear held up a calming paw.

"Leave, I said. Now. And don't come back until I call for you."

Rules were rules, a bargain had been struck, and the bear had said to leave. The alp magic'ed itself up and out the nearest window without so much as a spared look backward. It didn't need to look over its shoulder, it knew what it would see – that damnable bear with its crooked little mouth looking up at it with that sad serenity that had been sewn onto its face. No, best to just do as it was told, and leave. It wasn't like it could do anything else even if it wanted to – it was a fairy after all, and a deal is a deal.

"Dress," Fiona stated. She was hard at work writing something at the dining table behind her mother, Alice, as she fixed the pair some lunch.

"Code," her mother responded.

"Road," the little girl said. The game was one the two played often, with one party offering a rhyme, and the next responding with a close word associate.

"Trip," Alice said.

"Nip."

The woman looked up for a moment. "Tuck."

"Stuck?" Fiona asked more than said.

"Hmm," Alice stopped and bowed her head for a moment. She sighed, "I think you got me again."

Fiona looked up with a gapped grin. "Really?!"

"Really really," Alice smiled back. "You stuck me with 'stuck,' you little monster, how could you?" Fiona bubbled into a giggling fit that set Alice to laughing herself.

Just around the corner, our knight sat, sagged and silent as every stuffed friend should be. His black eyes shone with his warrior's focus as he waited patiently for the girls to settle back down into a comfortable quiet before Fiona started their game back up again. She was always in the mood for another round after a victory, of course, and the teddy bear was eager to continue his research into the wide world of meter and rhyme. After all – you never know when those sorts of things might come in handy.

Note: The Dream Eater wouldn't exist without the careful eye of my friend and collaborator Ian James Hackworth. Thank you, Ian.

Holly Walters originally hails from a small, rural, town in Minnesota. A life-long storyteller, Holly is also a cultural anthropologist with a PhD from Brandeis University working in the high Himalayas of Nepal. While her ethnographic work focuses on fossil folklores and sacred ammonites in South Asia, her creative work pays homage to the dragons, unicorns, and fairy tales of her youth. When not writing, she can be found perfecting her Medieval archery skills, theorizing about movie plots, and forgetting where she left her tea cup. Today, she makes her home in Boston, Massachusetts, with a very unruly garden, a few equally cantankerous pets, a clever spouse, and a resident house ghost. And since her creepy sculpture hobby hasn't panned out thus far, she is looking forward to the publication of her first novel and the writing of many more.

Adam Wassil isn't from any one place, but he'll call anywhere in the Midwest home comfortably enough. He's spent more time and money on school than he should have, but while he was there, he met some good people and found out he could add "writing prose and poetry" to the list of things he's passionate about, right alongside the tabletop and video-games, comic books, good food, coffee, and cartoons. He didn't get into art until his late 20's, early 30's, and the only reason he did was to maybe make a comic book of his own one day. He prefers working in pencil, pen, and ink, but he's been working digitally almost exclusively in more recent years.